TALES OF THE

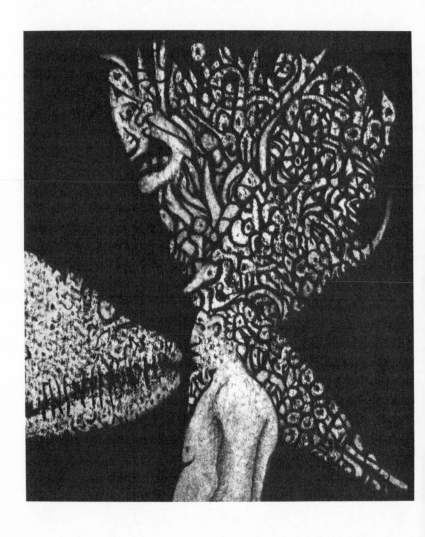

QUINTANA ROO

STORIES BY
James Tiptree, Jr.

ILLUSTRATED BY
Glennray Tutor

ARKHAM HOUSE PUBLISHERS, INC.

ACKNOWLEDGEMENTS

"What Came Ashore at Lirios," copyright © 1981 by Davis Publications, Inc., for *Isaac Asimov's Science Fiction Magazine*, 28 September 1981 (first published as "Lirios: A Tale of the Quintana Roo").

"The Boy Who Waterskied to Forever," copyright © 1982 by Mercury Press, Inc., for *The Magazine of Fantasy and Science Fiction*, October 1982.

"Beyond the Dead Reef," copyright © 1982 by Mercury Press, Inc., for *The Magazine of Fantasy and Science Fiction*, January 1983.

Composed in Albertus by Pendragon Graphics, Beaverton, Oregon.

Library of Congress Cataloging-in-Publication Data

Tiptree, James.
 Tales of the Quintana Roo.

 Contents: A note about the Mayas of the Quintana Roo — What came ashore at Lirios — The boy who water-skied to forever — [etc.]
 1. Fantastic fiction, American.   I. Title.
PS3570.I66T3   1986   813'.54   85-18576
ISBN 0-87054-152-8 (alk. paper)

Printed in the United States of America
First Edition

TO CARLOS ANTONIO GONZALES

KILLED AT FORTY-TWO BY PLANE CRASH
17 OCTOBER 1984; RECENTLY GOVERNOR
OF COZUMEL. FRIEND, HOST, AND TEACHER,
FISHERMAN AND NATURALIST, HIS DEATH
IMPOVERISHES THE QUINTANA ROO
AND ALL WHO KNEW HIM.

A NOTE ABOUT THE MAYAS OF THE QUINTANA ROO

The Quintana Roo—pronounced Keen-TAH-na Row—is a real and very strange place. It is the long, wild easternmost shore of the Yucatán Peninsula, officially but not psychologically part of Mexico. A diary of daily life on its jungly beaches could sometimes be taken for a log of life on an alien planet.

The Mayas who inhabit it extend in their millions, from Mexico down through Honduras and Guatemala and on south, and the differences between tribes and tribal language are often taken more seriously than "national" boundaries. The Mayas are the most oriental of all American Indians, but they do not have the oriental-doll delicacy. Along with the slant eyes go sloped-back foreheads and strong bones—and big hooked noses. The nose and the slant-back forehead are considered beauty marks, from their resemblance to serpents, and mothers used to tie boards on their babies' heads to slant them. A similar Maya beauty mark is crossed eyes; they are all, especially the babies, as cross-eyed as Siamese kittens—and again mothers used to tie a little ball of wax over a baby's nose to focus its eyes in. Another feature, which I cannot confirm personally—Mayas are modest—is the Maya Blue Spot said to be exhibited by the ladies just at the ends of their spines.

It is difficult for one struck by Mayaphilia to shut off, but perhaps the reader will permit me one last general observation: Mayas are barely "conquered" and often do not regard themselves as such. They are as different from the tribally-mixed, oft-enslaved Indians of mainland Mexico as an unreconstructed Highland Scot is from a forelock-tugging, class-conscious Londoner. None of this "Sí, sí, Señor" snake-oil. They look you straight in the eye from babyhood on, and demand to know what you're doing there. On the Quintana Roo coast today there are still (as of 1984) villages that exercise their treaty rights of remaining unassimilated and unmodernised. They are visited by invitation only. The former governor was a friend of mine, and when he made his ceremonial visit to such villages he went alone and did the last twenty kilometres on foot, using an old *sac bé* road. (The *sac bé* network is the road-system of Maya antiquity, now limestone ridges running through the jungle, some to no one knows where.)

The visitor who wants to understand the Yucatán, and why certain things are referred to as "Yucatecan" rather than "Mexican," should know that quite recently the Mayas rose and fought bloodily for their independence, mainly against Mexico. And the U.S.A. – that's us – sent troops to help Mexico. Thus until quite lately, and perhaps even today in some places, it was very important, when a wrecked sailor or lost hiker suddenly found himself surrounded by small mahogany men with slant eyes and three-foot *machetes*, to stress that he was NOT *Yanqui*, but preferably British. (The British helped the Mayas.)

The wars ended in 1935, not with a surrender but with a negotiated truce. The recency of the whole thing was brought home to me when I learned that the secretary-general of the Maya Armies died only the year I first went down there. Afterwards, Mexico promptly divided the peninsula into three parts: the provinces of Yucatán and Campeche, and the Territory of the Quintana Roo. (A territory is approximately what our Alaska used to be; Mexico has another over in Baja California.) The Quintana Roo became a province ten years ago, for administrative purposes. It is named for their hero of the Independence, Andrés Quintana Roo, whose fine head in bronze surveys the Cozumel *zócalo* today. Had the Mayas, like the Scots and the North Amerinds before them, been a bit less interested in settling ancient feuds and more able to unite against the common enemy, the national maps of the region from Campeche southward might be rather different today.

The present uniqueness of the Quintana Roo will, of course and alas, go under the incoming flood of Western and *gringo* ways. But one finds here and there an interest in reclaiming the millennial Maya culture. And beneath the surface, flow tides and ancient currents of great power. Most of the matter of the stories set down here is simple fact. And of the fiction remaining, who could swear it was not carried in the four-thousand-year-old voices that whisper and murmur in the nights of the Quintana Roo?

JAMES TIPTREE, JR.

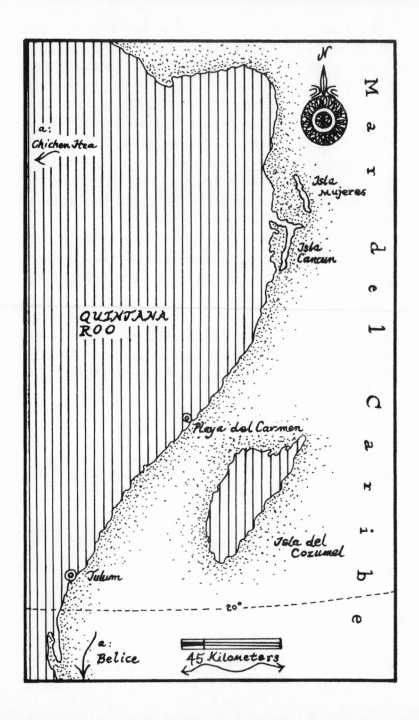

Tales of the Quintana Roo

The tourists throw spent Polaroid
Where Spaniards threw spent slaves;
And now and then a tourist joins
Five centuries of graves.
For love it's wiser to avoid
Smiles from those brilliant waves.

What Came Ashore at Lirios

The old coco-ranch foreman saw him first.

It was a day of roaring hot south wind. The beach smoked under the thrashing coco-palms, and the Caribbean raved by like a billion white devils headed for Cuba, four hundred miles north. When I went down to see what Don Pa'o Camool was peering at, I could barely hold one eye open against the glaring, flying sand.

The beach stretched empty to the hazed horizon: dazzling white coral marked only by faint hieroglyphs of tar and wrack.

"*¿Qué?*" I howled above the wind-shriek.

"*Caminante.*"

Interested, I peered harder. I'd heard of the *caminantes*, the Walking Men of old days, who passed their lives drifting up and down this long, wild shore. One of the dark streaks was, perhaps, moving.

"*¿Maya caminante?*"

The old man—he was a decade younger than I—spat down hard at a ghost-crab blowing by. "*Gringo.*" He took a hard sideways squint up at me, as he always did when he used that word.

Then he screwed his face into one of his wilder Maya grimaces, which might mean anything or nothing, and stumped back up the bluff to his lunch, slapping his big old-fashioned *machete* as he went.

My eyes were caked with salt and sand. I too retired up to my wind-eroded patio to wait.

What finally came plodding into view along the tide-line was

a black skeleton, a stick-figure with fuzz blowing around the head. When he halted by the compass-palm and turned to look up at the *rancho*, I half expected the sea-glare to shine through his ribs.

The *rancho* was a straggling line of five small pole-and-thatch huts, three smoky copra-drying racks, and a well with a winch-bucket. At the end was a two-room owner's *casita*, on whose rented patio I sat.

The apparition started straight up toward me.

Nearer, I saw he was indeed a *gringo*: the hair and beard whipping his sun-blackened face was a crusted pinkish grey. His emaciated body was charred black, with a few white scar-lines on his legs, and he was naked save for a pair of frayed shorts and his heavy leather sandals. A meagre roll of *serape* and a canteen were slung on his shoulders. He could have been sixty or thirty.

"Can I have some water, please?"

The English came out a bit rusty, but it was the voice that startled me: — a clear young voice right out of Midwest suburbia.

"Of course."

The sun glittered on a shark-knife hanging from the stranger's belt, showing its well-honed edge. I gestured to a shady spot on the patio curb and saw him slumped down where I could keep an eye on him before I went in. Incongruous young voices like his aren't unknown even here; they come from the scraps of human flotsam that drifts down the tropic latitudes hoping that tomorrow, or next year, they will get their heads in order. Some are heart-breaking; a few are dangerous, while they last. I knew that slant eyes were watching from the *rancho*—but no one could see into the *casa* and only a fool would rely on

a Maya to protect one old *gringo* from another.

But when I came out he was sitting where I'd left him, gazing out at the blazing mill-race of the sea.

"Thank you . . . very much."

He took one slow, shaky sip, and then two more, and sat up straighter. Then he uncapped his canteen, rinsed, and filled it carefully from my pitcher before drinking more. The rinse-water he poured on my struggling casuarina seedling. I saw that the canteen under its cooler-rag was a sturdy anodised Sealite. The knife was a first-rate old Puma. His worn sandals were in repair, too; and wearing them was a mark both of status and sense. When he lifted the glass again, the eyes that glanced at me out of his sun-ravaged face shone a steady, clear, light hazel.

I picked up my own mug of cold tea and leaned back.

"*Buut ka'an,*" the young stranger said, giving it the Maya click. "The Stuffer." He jerked his wild beard at the brilliant gale around us, and explained, between slow sips, "They call it that . . . because it blows until it stuffs the north full, see . . . and then it all comes blasting back in a Northeaster."

A scrap of my typing paper from the local dump came flittering by. He slapped a sandal on it, smoothed it, and folded it into his pack. As he moved, a nearby palm-root suddenly reared up and became a big iguana. The creature stared at us over its wattles with the pompous wariness that had carried it from the Jurassic, gave two ludicrous intention-bobs, and streaked off at a flying waddle, tail high.

We both grinned.

"More water?"

"Please. You have good water here." He stated it as a known fact, which it was.

"Where did you fill your canteen?"

"Pájaros. Punta Pájaros. Ffah!"

I refilled the pitcher, more than a little appalled. All ground-water quits at the lagoon-mouth a kilometre south. Even considering that he was walking north, with the wind, had this man, or boy, really come the thirty miles of burning bone-dry sandbar between here and the Pájaros lighthouse on that canteen? Moreover, Pájaros itself has no water; the fishermen who camp there occasionally bring in an oil-drum full, but were otherwise believed to subsist on beer, tequila, and other liquids not usually considered potable. No wonder he had rinsed the canteen, I thought, hunting out my pack of sodium-K tabs. Even without the Stuffer blowing, people can desiccate to congestive heart-failure without feeling it, on this windy shore.

But he refused them, rather absently, still staring at the sea.

"All the electrolyte you need, right there. If you're careful. Our blood is really modified sea-water . . . isn't that right?"

He roused and turned round to look at me directly, almost appraisingly. I saw his gaze take in the corner of the room behind us, where my driftwood bookshelves were dimly visible through the glass sliding doors that had long ceased to slide. He nodded. "I heard you had a lot of books. *Muy pesados*—heavy books. *Libros sicológicos.* Right?"

"Um."

This chance visitation was changing character unwelcomely. It wasn't odd that he should have known much about me—gossip has flowed ceaselessly up and down this coast for three thousand years. Now I had the impression that something about those "heavy psychological books" had drawn him here, and it made me uneasy. Like many experimental psychologists, I have had harrowing difficulties trying to explain to some distressed stranger that an extensive knowledge of the cognitive behaviour of rats has no clinical applications.

But his own radar was in excellent shape. He was already wrapping his canteen and slinging on his roll.

"Look, I don't mean to interrupt you. The breeze is easing off. It'll be nice later on. If you don't mind, I'll just go down by that big driftlog there and rest awhile before I move on. Thanks for the water."

The "breeze" was doing a roaring thirty knots, and the huge mahogany timber down on the beach could hardly be seen for flying sand. If this was a ploy, it was ridiculous.

"No. You're not interrupting anything. If you want to wait, stay here in the shade."

"I've snoozed by that log before." He grinned down at me from his skeletal height. His tone wasn't brash, just gentle and resolute; and his teeth were very white and clean.

"At least let me pass you a couple of spare grapefruit; I've more than I can eat."

"Oh, well, great . . ."

Looking back, it's hard to say when and why it began to seem important that he stop and not go on. Certainly my sense of him had changed radically about that time. I now saw him as competent to this country, and to his strange life, whatever it might be; doubtless more competent than I. Not flotsam. And not in need of any ordinary help. But as time went on, something—maybe a projection of my own, maybe the unrelenting wind-scream that day—perhaps merely the oddness of the sea-light reflected in his pale eyes—made me sense him as being, well, *marked*. Not at all "doomed"—which isn't uncommon in this land, particularly if one neglects to contribute to the proper officials. And not "scarred" as by some trauma. Or watched by an enemy. I had merely an unquieting sense that my visitor was at this time in some special relation to a force obscure and powerful, that he was significantly vulnerable to—I knew not what, only that it waited ahead of him, along the lonely sand.

But his talk, at first, couldn't have been less ominous. Stowing the wizened grapefruit, he told me that he came down every year to walk this coast. "Sometimes I get as far as Bélizé, before I have to start back. You weren't here when I passed going south."

"So you're on your way home now. Did you make Bélizé?"

"No. The business went on too late." He jerked his beard in the general direction of Yankeedom.

"May I ask what the business is?"

He grinned, a whimsical black skeleton. "I design swimming pools in Des Moines. My partner does most of the installation, but he needs my designs for the custom jobs. We started in college, five years back. It really took off; it got so heavy I had to get away. So I found this place."

I poured myself some more stale tea to let that sink in. Would my scrap of paper end as a sketch for some good citizen's Iowa patio?

"Do you ever run into any of the old *caminantes*?"

"Only a few left, old men now. Hidden Star Smith—Estrella Escondida Camal. Camol, Camool, it's like Smith here, you know. He stays pretty close to Pájaros these days. And Don't Point at Rainbows."

"I beg your pardon?"

"Another old *caminante*, I don't know his name. We were watching this storm pass at sunset, see? Maybe you've noticed —they can throw this fantastic double, triple *arco iris*. Rainbows. First one I'd seen. I pointed at it, and he got excited and clouted my arm down. '¡No puncte!'—don't point, see!" He rubbed his elbow reminiscently. "He doesn't speak much Spanish, but he got it to me that something bad would jump out of the rainbow and run down my arm right into my ear. So whenever I meet him I tell him 'No puncto,' and we have a laugh."

My visitor seemed to be enjoying talking to someone who knew a little of this shore, as his Des Moines clients would not. But his gaze still roved to the gale-torn sea, and he had not unslung his blanket-roll.

"How do you get across those two monster bays between here and Bélizé? Surely you can't hike around? Or have they finally cut back there too?"

"Not yet. No way. What isn't under water is tribal treaty land. I saw an air photo with three unnamed villages on it. I know where a couple of *sac bés* come out, though—you know, the old Maya roads. They're nothing but limestone ridges now. There was this man on one of them one night, he wasn't wearing pants. He disappeared like—whht! . . . I wanted to walk back in a ways this trip, but—" His gaze turned away again, he frowned at the wind. "I hated to get so far . . . inland."

"So, how do you cross?"

"Oh, I work my way on a fishing boat, fixing stuff. It's unreal, what this climate does to engines. They keep them going on string and beer. I have a couple of guys who watch for me every year. If I could only leave a set of tools, but—"

We both knew the answer to that one.

"Sometimes they take me all the way, or they drop me at Punta Rosa and I walk down and catch another ride over Espíritu Santo."

I asked him about the rather mysterious stretch of coast between the two huge bays.

"The beach is mostly rocks; you have to watch the tide. But there's an old jeep track up on the bluff. Five, no, let's see— six coco plantings. And the Pickle Palace, you know about that?"

"You mean it really exists?"

"Oh, yes. This incredible *rico-rico politico* from Mexico. The pickles were just a sideline. I guess he wanted a private paradise. Turrets, stained glass windows, at least a dozen guest-houses, everything tiled. An airstrip. And every damn bit brought in by lighter, through the reef. They say he went down a couple of times but his mistresses didn't like it. Of course it's all over-grown now. There's an old caretaker who chops it out and grows corn by the fountain. The thing is, the whole place is in exquisite taste. I mean really lovely. Nineteen-thirties art deco, top grade."

The incongruous words from this wild naked stranger—like the Pickle Palace itself—were eroding my sense of reality. This is not unusual in the Quintana Roo.

"And nobody seems to have looted the inside. I went in the kitchens, he had what has to be the first microwave oven in the world. Didn't stay long—there was a live tiger asleep in the living-room."

"You mean a jaguar?"

"No. A real tiger-tiger from India, with stripes. And huge. He must have had a zoo, see—there's birds that don't belong here, too. This tiger was on a white velvet couch, fast asleep on his back with his paws crossed on his chest, the most beautiful sight I ever saw. . . ." He blinked and then added quietly, "Almost."

"What happened?"

"He woke up and took off right over my head out the door." My guest grinned up, as if still seeing the great beast sail over. "Of course I was down, crawling like a madman out the other way. I never told anybody. But when I came by a couple years

later there was his skull speared up on the wall. Pity."

"That's a lovely story."

"It's true."

His tone made me say quickly, "I know it is. That's why it's good; made-up yarns don't count. . . . Look, this wind isn't going to quit soon. Maybe you'd like to come in and wash up or whatever while I scare us up a snack. Tea suit you, or would a Coke or some *cerveza* go better?"

"That's really good of you. Tea's fine."

As he followed me in he caught sight of his reflection in the sandy glass, and gave a whistle. Then I heard a clank: he had quickly unstrapped the knife and laid it down inside the sill.

"You really are *buenos gentes*, you know?"

I pointed out the old gravity-feed shower. "Don't get too clean, it'll draw the *chiquitistas*."

He laughed—the first carefree young sound I'd heard from him—and started turning out his pockets, clearly intending to walk straight under, shorts and all.

I put the kettle on my gas one-burner and started loading a tray with cheeses and ham. He came out just as I was pouring, and I nearly dropped the kettle on us both.

His skin was still burnt black, showing several more scars where he had apparently tangled with a coral-reef. The wet shorts were still basically khaki, but now visibly enlivened by sturdy Mexican floral-print patches, and edged top and bottom by pink lines of less-burnt skin. The effect was literally and figuratively topped off by his damp, slicked-down hair and beard: relieved of their crust, they shone and flamed bright strawberry red, such as I've seldom seen in nature—or anywhere else.

He seemed totally unconscious of the change in his appearance, and was looking carefully around the kitchen corner and my wall of books.

"You like stories?" he inquired.

"Yes."

"For a taste of that real maple-syrup up there I'll swap you a good one. I mean, true. I want to ask you a question about it."

I was too occupied reassembling the tray and my perceptions to indulge in any more suspicions, and answered simply, "With pleasure."

He watched appreciatively as I poured a generous dollop into a baggie and secured it in a sea-scoured *detergente* jar. "You scrounge the beach, too. . . ."

"My *supermercado*," I told him.

"That's right." His gravity was returning. "Everything you need . . . it sends."

When we'd got ourselves settled I saw that the Stuffer really was subsiding slightly. The coco-palms swept the sand in a wind which had lost a decibel or two; and the sea beyond was regaining some of its wondrous Carib turquoise, shot with piercing lime-green in the coral shallows. The white lemmings of the bay raced northward still; but the far reef was now visible as a great seething tumbling snow-bank, lit with the diamonds of the afternoon sun. It might be a nice night.

"It began right out there by your north point, as a matter of fact," my guest pointed left with his piece of cheese, and took a small bite. "This particular evening was fantastic — dead calm, full moon. You could see colours. It was like looking at a sunny day through a dark cloth, if you know what I mean."

I nodded; it was a perfect description.

"I was going along, watching the sea like I always do. You know there's an old pass through the reef out there? You can't see it now." He peered out to our left, absently laying down

the cheese. "Well, yes, you can if you know. Anyway, that's where I noticed this pole sticking up. I mean, first I saw it, and then I didn't, and then it bobbed up again, shining in the moonlight. I figured some idiot had tried to stick a channel-marker there. And then I saw it was loose, and wobbling along in the current. I guess you know there's about a three-knot current to the north all along here."

"I do. But look, eat first, story later. That cheese will die of old age."

I passed him some ham on a tortilla. He thanked me, took one big bite and laid it on his knee, his eyes still frowning at the reef, as though to recapture every detail.

"I slowed down to keep pace with it. Every big swell would wash it in closer. It kept almost disappearing, and then it'd come up again, bigger than before. For a while I thought it might be some huge fluorescent tube—you know how they come in,

waving—but when it got inside the reef I saw no bulb could possibly be that big, and it had some sort of—something—on it. By this time it was free of the reef, and going along north at a pretty good clip. Just this big pole in the sea, swaying vertically along getting shorter and taller—maybe two metres at times. I stayed with it, puzzled as hell. By this time I figured it might be the spar of some buoy, maybe dragging a chain that kept it upright."

He broke off and said in a different tone, "That lad in the blue hat. He your boy?"

I peered. A familiar battered bright-blue captain's hat was disappearing over the dune beside the *rancho*.

"That's Ek. Our local *niño*." I tapped my temple in the universal gesture that means here, Child of God. "He's somebody's wife's sister's son by somebody's cousin. Sort of a self-appointed guard."

"He chased me off your well with a *machete* when I came by last year."

"I think he's harmless really. But strong."

"Yeah . . . Well, anyway, this thing, whatever it was, had me sort of fascinated. When it got hung up I'd sit down and wait until it went on again. I wanted it, see. If it was an instrumented buoy, maybe there'd be valuable stuff on it. I've heard of people getting return rewards— Aaah, no. That's just what I told myself. The truth is, I just *wanted* it. I had a feeling—maybe this sounds crazy—like it was meant for me. I don't tell this well. You know, something coming in from the sea all by itself, and you're all alone—"

"I know exactly what you mean. This tea-tray came in like that. I spent half a morning getting it, in a Nor'easter."

He nodded his amazing-coloured head and gently touched the fine wood of the tray, as if I had passed some test.

"Yeah. Anything you need . . . Well, by this time what tide there was was going out, and I saw that the thing wasn't coming any closer for a while. But we were about half-way to that point where there's a back-flow. What they call a point around here is about as flat as your hand, but this one really does shift the current. About ten miles on. Some crazy Yank tried to build a resort there. *Lirios*."

"Yes. The Lilies. I came here the year the government chased him out. Misuse of agricultural land, they called it. He seems to have left owing everybody. I imagine they cleaned him out pretty well first; he had great plans. Is anything left?"

"Just some foundations with nice tiling, and part of a construction trailer. Fellow called Pedro Angel from Tres Cenotes has his family there; he runs a one-bottle *cantina*. Among other things. The *pozo* is still fairly good. I was going to get my water there if you weren't here."

I shook my head, thinking of those extra miles. "Ek shouldn't have done that to you. I'll talk to Don Pa'o."

He glanced at me, Maya-wise. "Don't bother. I mean, it won't help. Thanks anyway. Look—are you sure you want to hear all this?"

"Very sure. But I wish you'd put that ham out of its misery; you've picked it up six times. Is there anything you'd rather eat?"

"Oh, no, this is great." Obediently, he took two small bites and drank some tea, looking for the moment like a much younger man, a boy. His eyes were still on the calming reef, where even I could now see the zig-zag of darker water that was the old pass. The tide was running out. A solitary cloud cast a rosy reflection on the glittering horizon, and the palms were quieting. It would be a beautiful night indeed—with, I now recalled, a fine full moon. I had long since planned to bed my visitor down on a hammock in my "study." Maya hospitality is no problem; every corner has its hammock-hooks, and most commercial travellers even carry their own nets.

"Anyway, there I was, with this thing making long, slow bounces, getting taller and shorter, and me following right along. This beach in the moonlight . . ." His voice softened; the face in its flaming frame was still a boy's—but shadowed now by deeper feeling.

"The moon had started down inshore, so that it really lit up the pole, and just about the time we got to Lirios I saw that the markings were something wrapped around it. When it came up high I could see sort of white bulges, and then some dark stuff started to drift loose and blow. At first I thought it was seaweed, and then I decided it was an old flag. And I hadn't seen it before because the chain, or whatever was weighting it, held it down in deep water. But now it was dragging on the shallows, riding much higher out. And then it stuck on the Lirios sand-bar; and I saw it was a long thin bundle, wrapped or tied on the pole. It stuck there until a swell turned it around and carried it right toward me.

"And I saw the face."

His own face had turned sea-ward now, so that I had to lean toward him to catch the blowing words.

"It was a person, see, or a—a body. Tied to that spar, with long black hair floating and a sort of white dress flapping out between the ropes, starting to dry whenever it stayed out of the sea. . . . The person had to be dead, of course. But I didn't stop to think much, after I saw the face. . . . It . . . the . . ." He swallowed. "Anyway, there's a rotten back-flow there. Even if they say there's no such thing as an undertow, it feels like one. A sea-puss. I was wading and stumbling out, see. It's steep, and rough gravel. Not like here. But I swim a lot."

I repressed a protest. The Yank who built Lirios lost four customers before he would believe the locals: the surf there is no place to swim, even on the calmest days.

"The first wave that lifted me up, I saw the thing wasn't a buoy at all; there was more stuff surfacing beside the spar. Next time I got a look, I saw gunwales, and the top of a cabin astern. A fancy long-boat, see, maybe eight or ten metres. And polished—I could see the moon on wood and brass. The—the person was tied on the broken-off mast."

He took another mouthful of cold tea, his eyes on an inner vision. He seemed to be making an effort to recount this very carefully and undramatically.

"Polished . . ." He nodded to himself, yes. "Wet wood might look shiny, but not those oarlock things. Hell, I *felt* it, too! I'd got there, see, not even thinking. I mean, I'd never touched any dead people. Not really *dead*-dead. Just my grandfather's funeral, and his casket had glass. This was a lot different. I thought about what really dead fish were like, and I almost turned back. And then the next wave showed me the face close, and the eyes—her eyes were open. By then I was sure it was a woman. Her eyes seemed to be looking right at me in the bright moonlight. Shining—not dead. So huge . . . and her arm moved, or floated, like it was pulling at the ropes. So I kept on."

His hand instinctively moved to touch the knife he'd laid beside him.

"My leg hit something on the side of the boat beside her— that's where I got that one." He indicated a long grey scar. "And I started cutting ropes, all in among this silky stuff. The boat rolled us under water. I remember thinking, 'Oh, god, I'm cutting into dead meat; maybe she'll come all apart.' And the boat rolled worse; it was hung up on its keel, trying to go turtle." He drew a long breath. "But then her arm hit me and it felt firm. So I got a good grip on it and took another lungful of air, and cut the footropes way down under, and kicked us both out of there just before the whole thing rolled." He sucked in another lungful, remembering.

"After that it was just a battle. All that damn silk, and I can still see the moon going round and round through it; and I couldn't get any decent air at all, until a lucky wave rolled us up on that sliding gravel stuff. It isn't like here. I knew I had to get us farther up fast before the backwash. I caught one good look at this face, with the dark hair streaming over it. Her eyes were closed then. I sort of passed out for a minute; but I couldn't quite, because I knew I had to do something about the water in her. But all I could do was grab her waist—

a word. Among everything else, she was letting god know what she thought of him, too.

"You know they say down here the Spanish is five hundred words, and four hundred are curses. She used up the ones I knew in a minute or so and went on from there. I began to understand better—a lot about *oro, pozo dorado*, fountain of gold; and about her crew. She was pacing then, every so often I could hear her stamp. I pieced together that they'd found something, gold or treasure maybe—and her crew had deserted and left her tied on the boat. Or maybe they'd hit a rock in a storm—it was all pretty confusing. There was a lot about fighting, very violent. Maybe she'd tied herself on when she was alone in the storm. It sounded unreal, but real, too—I mean, I'd cut those ropes. And now she was asking—no, she was *telling* god exactly how to punish everybody. I think she was partly talking to the devil, too. All in the most graphic detail, you couldn't imagine—talk about bloody-minded—"

His lips still smiled, but his eyes were wide and sober, staring north up the beach.

"I lay listening to her, and picturing her in my mind. Like a woman out of Goya, you know? —Someone I'd never believed existed. Then I got my eyes open—it was bright, blazing moon-light, everything glittered—and I rolled over to see. Oh, god.

"I was looking up straight into this beautiful furious face—big black eyes actually flashing; scornful, utterly sensuous curled lips and nostrils—talk about aristocratic. She'd pulled her hair back and tied it. But then I saw the rest of her. It was all wrong. My woman was gone. The person was a man."

He shook his head slowly from side to side, eyes closed as if to shut out some intolerable sight, and went on in a flat, controlled tone.

"Yeah. He was younger than me, no beard. What I'd thought was a dress was this great white silk shirt, he was stuffing it back in his pants while he cursed and paced. Shiny tight black britches, with this horrible great fly, cod-piece, whatever, right in my face. He had loose soft black boots, with heels, and tiny feet. Ah, Christ, if I had the strength I'd have dragged him right back into the Caribbean and left him on that boat, I wanted my woman back so bad. . . .

"Then he noticed I was awake. His only response was to wind up one terrifying curse, and say '*Vino*' at me. Not Hello or what—just '*Vino*,' without hardly looking at me. Like I was some kind of a wine-machine. And paced off again. When he turned back and saw I hadn't moved, he glanced at me sharper and repeated '*Vino!*' quite loud. I still wasn't moving. So he came a step nearer and said, '*Entonces. Agua.*'

"I just stared up at him. So he snapped his fingers, like he was talking to a dog or an idiot, and said very clearly, '*¡A-gua! Agua para tomar.*'

"You never saw arrogance like that. To get his point over, he flipped the empty canteen over in the sand toward me with the toe of his boot. That really pissed me off, getting sand on the screw-threads. I had him figured for some zillionaire general's spoiled brat, playing games. I started getting up, not really sure whether I was going to murder him or just walk away. But I found I was so weak that standing up was about it for me then. So I remembered this thing a lady had put me down with, and wrestled it into my best Spanish.

" 'The word you're groping for, man, is thank you.'

"It must have sounded like some weird dialect to him, but he got the point of that '*hombre*.' Oh, wow! Did you actually ever see anyone's nostrils flare with rage? And the mad eyes—

it was tiny, I could almost touch both hands around — and kind of jolt her face-down as I crawled up the shingle on my knees. A gush of water came out. And then we both fell into the trash-line, and there was my canteen. So I managed to pour some fresh water more or less at her mouth through the hair, and I thought her eyes were opening again just as I passed out for good. . . . Funny," he added in a different tone, and frowned.

"What?" I was frowning too, wondering how strong those skeleton tendons could be. A formidable feat, if true. But he was not, after all, much thinner than Cousteau, and a lot younger. And the Quintana Roo is peopled with survivors of harrowing ordeals.

"The trash-line was different," he said slowly. "No *basura*, no kipple at all — just a little natural tar, and weed and sea-fans, you know. I can see it." He screwed up his eyes, remembering hard for a moment.

"Anyway," he went on, "I was out cold, I don't know how long. The next thing I remember is hearing that voice." His lips twitched in a dreamy grin.

"It was a perfectly beautiful voice, soft and rough-low — contralto, d'you call it? — going on and on. I just lay still awhile, listening. She was standing up somewhere behind my head. This incredible emotion! And complicated too. Controlled. I couldn't make out the language, although I heard '*Dios*' a few times. And then I caught the lisp: *ththth*. *Thetheo*, what they call Castilian. I'd heard it once on a tape, but never like this. At first I thought she was thanking god for saving her." His grin flickered again.

"She was cursing. Swearing. Not like a *puta*, no simple stuff, but this long-cadence, complex, hissing fury. So intense — I tell you it was so savage it could scorch you if you didn't know

you wouldn't believe. His right hand whipped around and hit a scabbard I hadn't noticed—lucky for me it was empty. I could see the gold jewel-work on it glitter in the moonlight. That gave him a minute to look me over hard.

"I guess I puzzled him a little, when he came to look. I was a lot huskier then, too, and my gear was in better shape. Anyway, he stayed real still in a sort of cat-crouch, and said abruptly, '*Inglés.*'

" 'No,' I told him. '*Estados Unidos del Norteamérica.*'

"He just shrugged, but the edge was off his rage. He repeated more calmly, extra-clear, 'I desire more water. Water to drink.'

"I was still mad enough to say, 'More water—*please.*'

"Man, that nearly sent him off again; but he was still studying me. I was bigger than him, see, and he didn't know I was about to fall down if he pushed. I saw his eyes flicking from my hair to my knife to this big flashy diver's watch I wore. By luck the thing did one of its beeps just then, and his fantastic eyebrows curled up and met, in the moonlight. Next second he gave a chuckle that'd curl your hair, and suddenly bent and swept me an elaborate bow, rattling off the most flowery sarcastic speech you ever heard—I could only get parts, like 'Your most gracious excellency, lord of the exalted land of hell-haired lunatics,' and so on, ending with a rococo request for water. The word 'please' was of course nowhere in it. No way.

"Would you believe, I started to like the little son-of-a-bitch?"

My visitor turned to look straight at me for a moment. The blaze of the calming sea behind him made a curly fire of that beard and hair, and there was a different look in his hazel eyes. I recognised it. It's the look you see in the eyes of men from Crooked Tree, Montana, or Tulsa, or Duluth, when you meet them sailing the Tasman sea, or scrambling up some nameless mountain at the world's end. The dream—faintly self-mocking, deadly serious dream of the world. *Farther*, it says. *Somewhere farther on is a place beyond all you know, and I shall find it.* It had carried this boy from Iowa to the wild shore of Yucatán, and it would carry him farther if he could find the way.

"—maybe it was just his *macho*," my visitor was saying. "I mean, the little bastard had to be half-dead. And his crazy get-up, and the *pozo dorado* business. For some reason I figured he might be from Peru; there's some pretty exotic super-rich types down there. But it was more than that. More like he'd found a key to some life way out, free—something neat. I mean really far off, far away, *lejos*. . . ."

His own voice had become far-off too, and his eyes had gone back to the sea. Then he blinked a couple of times and went on in his normal tone.

"He misunderstood my standing there, I guess. 'I will pay

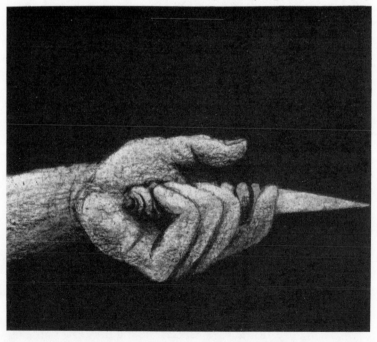

you,' he told me. *'Pagaré. Gift. Te regalaré. ¡Mira!'*

And before I could find words he had reached down and slapped one boot-heel, and his hand came up with this wicked little three-inch stiletto on his thumb. His other hand was yanking up his shirt. The next thing, he was sticking this blade right in by his lowest rib.

"'Hey, man — No!' I sort of lurched to get his arm, but then I saw he was just slicing skin. Two big gouts came welling out. They fell on the sand, with only a little blood — and they rolled! One of them flashed deep green in the moonlight, deep green like the sea. He picked them up, with that thumb-sticker pointed straight at me, and looked them over critically. The green one he dropped into his boot somewhere, and the other one he held out to me. It was dark, about as big as a small marble, lying on this slender pointy-fingered hand.

"'A token of my estimation for your timely assistance.'

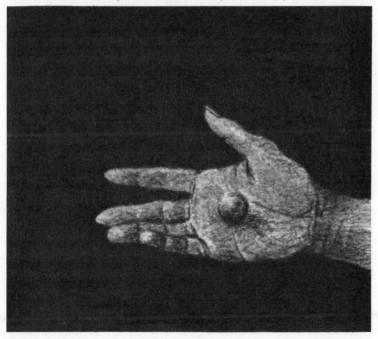

"When I didn't move, the palm began gracefully to tilt, to spill the stone on the ground. So I took it. Anybody would. Not meaning to keep it, you know, just out of curiosity, to see it close.

"It wasn't gem-cut, only polished-off cabochon, but when I held it up the moonlight showed through dark blood-red, like there was a fire inside. It had to be a ruby. If it wasn't too badly flawed, it must have been worth god knows what. I figured it was good, too; obviously he had chosen his best stuff to sew into his hide.

"My Spanish was drying up. I was trying to make up a suitably polite refusal and get the thing back into his hand, when I saw his eyelids sliding down, and his whole body sagged. He got himself straightened up again, but I could see him swaying, fighting to stay on his feet. Jesus, I got scared he was going to die in front of my face after what he'd been through.

"'Rest. I will bring water.'

"I had the sense not to touch him, even then. I just picked up the canteen, nearly falling over myself, and smoothed off a clean spot for him to settle onto. He sank down gracefully, resting his chin and arms on one knee, the knife still in his hand. The moon was starting down behind us, into the inland jungle, and its pitch-black shadow was spreading from the bluff to the beach where we were. I couldn't spot the trail up to Lirios. It's all low there, though, and I knew it had to be close, so I just started straight up the nearest gully.

"I needed both hands to haul myself up, so I stuck the ruby in my pocket." My visitor's hand went to his shorts. "The left back one, with the button." He nodded his head. Again I had the impression he was trying to recall every detail. "I remember I had a hell of a time securing it, but I knew I shouldn't lose

that. And then I went on up to the top of the rise. Wait—"
He clenched his eyes, saying almost to himself, "Coco-palms.
Did I see cocos there? . . . I don't know. But there aren't very
many; it's never been farmed. Just wild ones.

"When I hit the top, I found I'd made it wrong. There wasn't
any clearing, just a trail. But Lirios's damn radio goes twenty-
four hours a day; I knew I'd hear it soon. The night was dead
calm now, see; every so often I could hear a wave flop on the
beach below. So I staggered along north, stopping every few
steps to listen. I was feeling pretty low. If Pedro's radio was
off, there was no use looking for a light—he shuts up tight.
All I heard was a couple of owl hoots, and the moon getting
lower all the time. And dry—I tried to chew a palm-leaf, but
it only made me worse.

"I'd just about decided that I should have gone south—this
was only my second trip in there, see—when I saw a clearing
right ahead and there was this funny slurping sound. The moon
was shining on a kind of *ruina* by one side. I wondered if maybe
this was a secret *pozo*—people don't tell you everything, you
know. When I got about ten steps into the moonlight, a peccary
exploded out and tore off like a pint-size buffalo. It about scared
the pants off me, but I knew that slurping had to mean water.
So I went over to the stone blocks and stepped in a wet place.
This struck me odd at the time, because it was a dry year; the
lagoons even were low; but I didn't stop to worry about it. I just
crawled through till I found the hole, and stuck my head in
and guzzled. Then I filled the canteen and a plastic bag I had,
and got everything on me soppy wet, for that poor lad down
below. I remember thinking this would be a nice spot to camp
out for a couple days till we got our strength back, so I stood
up to orient myself. The moon was still on the *laguna* right

down below me, and I sighted on an islet with a big strangler fig. The lagoon was high here, but that didn't bother me—you know how this weather varies; one place can get soaked while the rest of the coast dries up. Then I cut straight up over the dune and more or less fell down to the beach, and went back south on the last edge of moonlight to where I'd left him.

"I found him easy; he'd had the sense to crawl to a patch of light before he collapsed. Now he was lying face-up, asleep or unconscious. I was scared for a minute, but his head was thrown back and I could actually see the pulse going by his long, full throat. The jaw-line was delicate, like a child's or a girl's, and those great soft black lashes on his cheeks made him look more than ever like a beautiful woman. I knelt down by him, wondering if it could possibly be. I'd only seen the bottom of his ribs, you know. And those stuffed pants could be a fake—people do crazy things. And I'd felt that tiny waist. I was just getting my nerve to pull the shirt up, when the lashes lifted and the huge dark eyes met mine.

"'*Agua pura.*' I held the canteen by his mouth. 'Drink—*tome.*'

"The hands made a feeble movement, but they were too weak to hold the canteen. I could see the fight was gone too; the eyes looked like a bewildered child's.

"'*Perdón,*' I said, just in case, and slid one hand carefully through that glossy mass of hair to join canteen and mouth.

"'Slowly. Drink slowly, *despacio.*'

"Obediently my patient took long, slow sips, breathing deeply and stopping now and then to stare up at me. Presently an innocent, beautiful smile came on the lips. I smiled back, realising that this stranger had in all probability decided that I had taken his gem and left him there to die. But just as my hand went to my pocket to give it back to him, his head fell back again across my arm. It was so heavy that I had to lie down alongside to support it, and the canteen was finished that way. I bathed the forehead and face with my wet bandanna, too.

"When I produced my plastic water-bag the smile changed to pure wonder, and the eyes grew wider still. Despite thirst, that transparent plastic had to be felt and poked at before my patient would drink. . . . I can remember how oval and shiny the nails were. Not polished, you know, but buffed in some way. And very clean; I could even see their white half-moons.

"The real moon was going down fast behind us. In the last light on the shore, I noticed that the long-boat had washed close in. She was riding heeled over, dousing that broken mast in and out with every quiet swell. It would have been a torturing end for someone tied there. I guess I shuddered.

"The person in my arms raised up enough to follow my gaze, and for a second I saw again the furious aristocrat. Saw and *felt* — it was like a jolt of voltage through my arms and chest. I didn't like the idea of what so much rage could do in a person so weak. By luck I had just located an old piece of health-bar in my shirt. It was sodden but okay, so I broke it and touched it to the stranger's lips.

"'*Es bueno. Come.*'

"A tongue-tip came out to explore the lips, dainty as a cat.

"'*¡Chocolate!*' My patient stared at me open-mouthed, the boat forgotten.

"'*Sí*, it's good. Eat some.'

"'*¡Chocolate!*' And the next thing I knew the stranger had stuffed the whole thing in his or her mouth, like a kid, with me trying to say 'Take it easy' and both of us grinning like mad.

"I recall thinking that chocolate couldn't be all that rare in

Peru or wherever. Was it possible the person I was holding in my arms was simply a refugee from some expensive nut-house?

"But there was one thing I was determined to find out, if I could just hold out until my companion went to sleep. It wouldn't be long now; another sip or two of water, and the furry lashes were sweeping low with fatigue. The only trouble was, I was almost asleep myself. And the darkness coming over us didn't help. Even the occasional muffled clanking from the boat was starting to sound like music. I wedged a sharp rock under my shoulder, and that helped a bit. The person in my arms was drifting off; I could feel the body softening and fitting against mine in a way that made me absolutely convinced it had to be a woman, or the damnedest gay earth ever created. But that rock was getting to feel soft. I was desperate enough to actually try pinching myself as hard as I could, with fingers that felt like Jello.

"The second time I did that, I hit the lump in my back pocket and remembered the ruby. That woke me a little; it seemed unbearable that this aristocrat might think the stone had bought that water. So I wriggled enough to unbutton and carefully pull it out. Or rather, I tried to. My fingers have never felt so clumsy. It was almost like the stone was hiding, it didn't want to come.

"But I finally managed to get hold of it and ease it across my body toward where one of his/her hands was lying on the sand beside the head. A star shone right through as I raised it. I guess a poet could find the right words, but the truth is that the only red flash I've ever seen like that was on a police squad-car.

"The hand was lying palm-up, with the fingers slightly curled, and I went to put the ruby in it. Again I had trouble. The hand moved but without moving, if I can describe it—maybe I was

just too dead to focus right. And that she-body was half under mine now, and it moved in a way that—well, you wouldn't have thought mine could respond, in the state I was in, but I did. That made me more than ever eager to get rid of that damned stone. I made three grabs at that little hand and caught the wrist, and forced the thing in her palm and curled her fingers over it, so I could get my own hand back where it wanted to be.

"But her body had slackened and fallen away from me, and before I could stop myself my nose went down in her cool dark hair and I was dead to the world.

"I didn't remember until next day that just at the very end, as I was folding her warm fingers, they seemed to change too, and turn kind of cold and stiff. And there was a strange faint sound from away on the sea, I guess it might have been a kind of wail from the boat's scraping, or like a bird's voice. . . ."

His own voice had grown cool and quiet.

"That's it, really."

He showed his teeth in a comfortless grin.

"I woke up in a blazing sunrise, all alone. There wasn't one mark on the beach, not even my own footprints. But lots of plastic trash now—there was a Clorox bottle by my head. It hadn't been there before. Maybe the tide sent up a little wavelet, enough to smooth everything out without waking me. It was far out again by then, farther than I've ever seen it. No sign of a boat, of course. I guess if this was a good ghost story, there'd have been *something*"—he gave that joyless grin—"but there wasn't a single trace. Not even one long black hair. I looked, you see. I looked. The only tiny thing was, my hip pocket was unbuttoned. Oh, how I searched. And all the while hearing Lirios's damn radio yattering from over the bluff."

He made a sound somewhere between a cough and a sigh.

"After . . . after a while I climbed up; the path was right behind me. When I looked back I noticed three or four dark knobs of wood sticking out of the water 'way far out, like in a line. . . . I bought some tacos off Pedro, and filled up the canteen on his skunk-water, with the radio banging out mariachis and tyre ads. The thing is, Pedro's *pozo*, his well, was right where the old *cenote*, the water hole, had been. I checked — it was the same view, but the water was low, like everywhere else that year. So I went back on the beach and walked on north. It was like a dream — I mean, not the other; the dream was Lirios and Pedro's *chistes* — joking. Or no, it was more like two dreams at once . . . ever since."

He was eyeing me intently, Maya-style, out of the corners of his clear *gringo* eyes. I got very busy discouraging some sugarants that were after his pack-roll.

"When I came by next year, you weren't around."

"No. I was late."

"Yeah. And I was earlier. . . . Nobody was around but some kids and that lad with the *machete*."

He nodded his beard at Ek, who had resumed surveillance at extreme range.

"When I got by Lirios there were five *borrachos* from the Guardia Nacional roaring up and down the beach on their new Hondas and firing handguns at the moon. So I went on by. About sunrise I met an old *ranchero* walking down from Tuluum. We talked awhile. A fine old guy, I gave him my plastic waterbag. Turned out he knew all about me — you know how it goes around here."

"*De veras*. I've never yet gone anywhere I wasn't expected."

"Yeah." He wasn't listening. "Anyway, he wanted to make sure I'd passed by Lirios at full moon the year before. When

I told him 'Yes,' he said, 'Good. In *la noche negra*, the moon-dark, the very bad ones come. Not often, you understand— but they *can*.' Then he asked me if anybody had given me anything there.

"I told him, 'No, at least, I didn't keep it.' He looked at me real hard and serious. '*Bueno*,' he said. 'If you had kept it, you would be *perdido*—lost. So long as you touch or hold anything. And are you free now? It is much the best that you go by day. Do you know the name of that place?'

"'No.'

"'*El Paso de los Muertos*. The pass or place of the dead, their *querencia*. Because all things come to the shore there. From Ascensión, Morales, Jamaica even. Sometimes quite big *lanchas*, shrimp-boats even from the Gulf. The rocks turn the current under water, you see, very far out. People used to make *mucho dinero* from what came there. But only by day, you understand. Only in the light of the sun. That's all finished now. The Guardia Aéreo finds them first from their planes.' He pointed out east. 'Where the sea turns by the *rifé de Cozumel*. Only wood and *basura*, worthless things come now.'

"'I think I saw the ribs of one old wreck. The tide was very far out.'

"'Ah?' He gave me that penetrating stare again. 'It must have been indeed very low water,' he said. 'Only once, in my youth, have I seen such a thing. I waded out to see it—in the day. It had been a sailing-boat. You know the metal *grimpas* used to hold the mast-ropes?' He did a little sketch in the sand, show- ing the stays. 'These were not fitted in, my friend, the way they do today. They were made of hot metal, poured right into the side of the ship. Which has not been done for two, three hundred years.'"

My visitor gave a deep sigh, or shudder, and tried the grin again.

"Anyway, we said goodbye and went our ways, and when I got to Tuluum I heard that something had happened to one of the drunk *soldarero* kids the night before. I found out later that Pedro's brother dragged the Honda out of the drink and filed off all the numbers. He's trying to fix it up."

Abruptly, the light eyes locked on mine. I couldn't dodge.

"Look. *Is it* possible?" He nodded at the shelves behind the glass. "You're supposed to know things. Aren't you? Could I have, well, *dreamed* all that? I mean, it went on so long—it started right over there, you know. I must have walked after that thing for ten miles."

His voice got low and slow, the words almost forced out.

"Could I have—made it up? Believe me, I'm not a day-dreamer, I don't even dream much at night. And I don't drink, only a few beers. No grass for years now. And the other shit they have down here, I learnt not to mess with that the first week I was here. And fiction, movies, mystic stuff—forget it. Here, look—" He bent and fished a thick pamphlet out of his pack. It was titled *Hydraulic Properties of Natural Soil Aggregates*. He put it back and looked straight up at me.

"Am I—crazy? How could I have made up all that? Was I in a different time? *Am I crazy?* . . . What do you think?"

He was really asking.

I was thinking that I knew many people who would be delighted to take charge, to enlighten him on the ultimate nature and limits of reality, or the effects of dehydration and solitude on cerebral function. But some minutes earlier I had discovered I wasn't one of them. What in hell *did* I think, what had I been doing all during that long account, except believing him? . . .

I knew what I *should* think, of course. All too well I knew. But, well—maybe one can dwell too long on the sands of the Quintana Roo.

I started a tentative mumble when he interrupted me, almost whispering: "How could I have made up that song?"

"Song?"

"I—I guess I didn't tell you about that." His face had turned back toward the sea, so that all I could catch from the fading gusts of the Stuffer was something about "at the end, see . . . and even this year."

He coughed again, and began to hum tunelessly, and finally sang a phrase or two, still watching the far reefs. His voice was clear and pleasing, but totally off any conceivable key.

"You see?" He glanced briefly at me. "I can't sing *at* all. So how could I . . . ? I can hear it, though."

The tune he had produced could have been any of a hundred Spanish wails—*amorado, corazón de oro, amor dorado lejos, lejos por la mar*—*Quisiera viajar;* that sort of thing: love, golden love far over the sea, who would not journey to the golden heart of the sea? . . . If there was anything extraordinary there, my Spanish could not detect it. Yet it seemed to have significance for him, as sometimes the most ordinary phrases do, in our dreams. Could I salvage my own sanity by hinting at this?

But whatever I might have said, I had delayed too long. His gaze was on the sea again, and he spoke in a whisper, not to me.

"No. I didn't make up that song."

Our moment had passed. Abruptly, he was on his feet, picking up his pack and canteen. The sea was almost calm now, a burnished splendour of green-gold and salmon, flushed with unearthly lavender and rose, reflections of the tropic sunset behind us. My dismayed protests blended with his farewell.

"Please wait. I'd assumed you'd spend the night here. I have a good spare *amaca*."

He shook his flaming head, smiling politely.

"No. But thanks for the stuff and everything, I mean, really."

"Can't you wait a moment? — I meant to give you some —"

But he was already moving away, turning to stride down the beach. My last view of his expression was a mingled eagerness and sadness, a young face shadowed by a resolution I couldn't hope to break. The sunset behind us was now filling the air with golden haze, the palms were still.

After a moment I followed him down to the beach, irresolute. His easy stride was deceptive; by the time I reached the tide-line his thin figure was already filmed by the soft twilight air between us. Even to catch him now I would have to run. The mad notion of accompanying him on his walk through the night died before the reality of the old heart jittering in my ribs.

I could only stand and watch him dwindle, fade into the stick-figure I had seen at first. Tropic dusks come fast. By the time he was rounding the point I could barely make him out, had it not been for the occasional glint of his red hair. Just as he turned the corner of the mangroves a new light came from sea-ward and lit up his head with rosy fire. Then he was gone.

I turned and saw that the full moon was rising through the cloud-castles on the sea, a great misshapen ball of cold gaseous light. For a moment it shone clear, at the apex of its luminous sea-path; and the beach became a snow-scape in silver and black. Then the high clouds took it again, in racing patterns of lemon and smoky bronze; and I turned to make my way up to the dark *casa*. Automatically I registered the high cirrus from the east — tomorrow would be fine. As I neared the patio, Ek's hat scuttled behind a dune on the road. He too had been

watching the stranger go.

And that's it, really, as the strange boy said.

The night turned greasy-hot, so that about midnight I went down to cool myself in the placid sea. Mayas do not do this; they say that the brown sharks come close in on calm nights, to bear their young in the shallows. I waded out hip-deep to my sand-bar, wondering where my visitor was now. Great Canopus had risen, and in the far south I could just see Alpha Centauri, magnificent even in the horizon veils. The sheer beauty of the scene was calming. No wonder my young friend wanted to make his way by night. Doubtless he was already near Tuluum, perhaps curled up in one of his wayside nests, savouring a grapefruit, fighting off the *chiquitistas*.

The thought of the grapefruits had reassured me some time back. Surely a man does not set out to meet god knows what, to follow delusions or invoke spirits or yield to succubi—armed with two mediocre grapefruits and a baggie of maple-syrup?

But as I stood there in the quicksilver Caribbean, a triangular shadow with something large and dark below it caught my attention. Only a sea-fan, no doubt. But I decided it would be prudent to return to land before it came into the channel I had to cross. And as I splashed ashore another memory came back; my young friend claimed to have fed chocolate to his particular apparition. Was my maple-syrup possibly destined for the same?

This troubling notion combined with the extraordinary heat and heavy calm—effects not often met on this shore—and with an overactive conscience to give me a very bad hour on the patio that night. What had I done, letting him go on? Hallucinated or sane, it was equally bad. Several times I came within a gull-feather of rousing out Don Pa'o's son to ride me to Lirios on his bike. But what then? Either we would find nothing, or ignominiously come upon my young man eating Pedro's tacos. And either way, my hard-won reputation of being fairly sensible, for a *gringo*, would be gone for good. . . . I fear that selfishness, rather than good sense, drove me finally to my hammock and uneasy sleep. And in the fresh morning breeze, what passes for sanity prevailed.

The tale has no real ending, but only one more detail which may have no bearing at all.

The next week of fine weather saw me plunged back into some long-overdue paperwork, during which no gossip came by. And then the advent of the *rancho*'s first real live school-teacher threw everyone into a great bustle. She was a resolute and long-suffering Maya maiden, sent by the *Goberierno* to see that the *rancho*'s grandchildren did not grow up as wild as their parents had. I found myself involved in making peace between her and the owner, who paid one of his rare visits expressly to get her out. My task was almost hopeless, until the generator conveniently — and expensively — broke down, and I was able to convince him that it might be useful if someone could read the manual. Thus, with one thing and another, I found no occasion to query Don Pa'o about the *gringo caminante* before it was time for me to go.

The next year I came early, and found myself keeping one eye on the beach. Nothing came by, until there was a little excitement at Lirios: a body did wash ashore. But I quickly discovered it was the corpse of a small dark man with the name OLGA tattooed on his arm.

That evening was another windless one, and I strolled over to where Don Pa'o and his lady were dining alone in their outdoor kitchen. The last of their resident sons was staying in Cozumel that year, learning to lay bricks.

After the ritual greetings, I remarked that one was reminded of the red-haired *gringo* walker, who did not seem to have come by this year. As I spoke, the old man's mouth drew down, until he looked exactly like the petty Maya chieftain his grandfather had been.

"Do you think he will come this year?"

Don Pa'o shrugged, and the globular brown matron who had borne his ten children gave the all-purpose Maya matron's cackle, intended to convey nothing except possibly a low opinion of her conversant.

"Perhaps he has gone back to *Norteamérica*?" I persisted.

Don Pa'o squinted at me hard for an instant, and then his slant eyes drooped, and his chin swung slowly from shoulder to shoulder.

"*No*," he said with finality.

At the same moment his wife made an extraordinary complex criss-cross of one hand across her abdomen. It puzzled me, until I recalled that some of the high-status older ladies here profess a brand of Catholicism whose rites and dogmas would doubtless astonish the Roman church. Then she got up to take the plates.

I did not need another look at the old man's archaic face to know that the subject was closed—and to sense too that I would not be seeing the strange red-haired boy again.

But why? I thought, as I made my farewells. What do they, what can they know? I have enough casual informants along this coast to ensure that nothing really disastrous or sensational could have occurred without my catching at least an echo of it, after this long. Mayas love morbidity; the actual fact was probably that my young friend was minting money in the swimming pool business, or had decided to explore someplace else.

Yet as I sat on my moonlit patio, listening to the quiet splash of the wavelets on the beach below, they seemed to be sighing out the odd little tuneless tune my visitor had tried to sing. *Amor dorado lejos, lejos por la mar.* I realised I'd been half-hearing it now and again, particularly when I swam on quiet days, but I had put it down to the murmur in my bad ear. Now it was plainer. And the stranger's whole tale came back to me, as I had not let it do before. A year had passed and cooled; I could reflect.

I found I did not believe it—or rather, I did not believe in its outward detail and aspect. It could, I suppose, be some unquiet spirit who came to my young friend, some long-dead Spaniard or revenant *conquistador,* some androgynous adventurer proffering ghostly gold; a life-hungry succubus from the shadows between the living and the dead. Or he could have

been, very simply, out of his head. Yet I didn't quite believe that either.

What haunts me yet is the idea that something . . . did come to him there, something deeper than all these, which took on those manifestations to lure and seek him out. Something to which he was peculiarly vulnerable; and which, I fear, took him to itself on the night he left me. (For it has been five years now that he has not been here, and there is word that his partner in Des Moines has never seen him back.) What could it be?

I gazed out long at the impersonal beauty before me, scarcely daring to name it: the last great wonder of the world. . . . "Anything you need," the boy had said. Whimsical as a tea-tray, seductive as a ruby, more terrible than all the petty armies of man. Who could say what was not in it, despite all our tiny encroachments and sorties? Perhaps we will kill it. And with it, ourselves. But it is far from dead yet—and its life is ours. As the boy had said too, our blood is its very substance, moving in our veins.

As I prepared to cease gazing and go to my human sleep, I recalled a trivial detail which carried an odd conviction. The Spanish word *mar* has one extraordinary aspect: *El mar, la mar* —*sea* is the only word in Spanish, or any other tongue known to me, which is both female and male indifferently and alike. If it was indeed the Sea itself which came for my friend, is it any wonder that it came in double guise?

The deep dominions know her rule;
Her jewelled minions rove,
Where human still may trade a soul
For her unhuman love.
And the one she has accepted
May finish out the race
Through portals unsuspected
To another time and place.

The Boy Who Waterskied to Forever

This happened the year the coast road finally came through.

For eight years, a trail cut by *machete* and strewn with piano-sized rocks had run behind the coco ranch and ended at the *boca*, the inlet from lagoon to sea. Now the Yucatecan government had bridged the *boca* and pushed a one-lane cut all the way south to the fishing colony at Pájaros lighthouse. It was an evil deed.

Every evening now the big refrigerator trucks ground past, going south; in the small hours before dawn they came groaning back, loaded to the axles with illegal seafood—rare and delicious fish and stone-crabs, netted on the last spawning grounds of the bay for the greedy stomachs of the tourists a hundred miles north at the new resort of Cancún. No comfort that this traffic would not last long, for its end would mean that those species had been fished to extinction. Nightfall for another wild beauty.

But there was a tiny, selfish compensation: the new road did make it possible for an elderly bicycling *gringo* to reach a hitherto-inaccessible small bay. It was a magical, untouched diving paradise that I spotted from the air. Ferocious reefs barred it from the sea, and once-impenetrable mangrove swamps guarded it from the land. Twice this year I had cycled to the vicinity, laboriously hidden my wheel to avoid leaving tracks, and fought my way to shore, guided by the sound of the sea. But each time I had come too late to take more than a taste of Eden before I had to start my exhausting trek back to the *rancho*.

This day I started early enough. The sun stood just past noon when I stood on the rocky verge of the enchanting little cove. The water was four metres of crystal, revealing a rich undersea world. Three pink spoonbills stared incuriously from the far side as I shucked off shirt and pants, and a bananaquit investigated my shoes. There was no trace of other visitors or alien paths, and the snorkel gear I had hidden there last trip was all intact. I checked the papers and *dinero* already in their

waterproof pouch on my belt and slipped off the rocks into the warm Caribbean with great delight: here was a place where snorkelling was the perfect way to go, where I could forget that age had put solo scuba dives forever beyond my strength.

Those first hours fled like moments; the reality was even finer than the promise. I visited first my few familiar spots: the ledge where two enormous black angelfish had set up housekeeping—

and there they were, sweeping flat to the pale sand as my shadow came over, rolling their big eyes in what seemed like an imploring plea, but was doubtless considered menacing by their natural enemies. Then there were the tiny clouds of colour rising from where the brilliant parrot-fish munched and chewed a rock. And the white sand floor, which suddenly erupted into a four-foot stingray, sailing off to halt in frozen invisibility a few yards away. Obviously no one had ever used a spear-gun here.

Then I began to explore, letting the gentle swells carry me over perfect lace-coral fields, dazzled by neon-blue angels, admiring the impossible pink of the ill-named and delectable hog-fish—another proof, if one were needed, that no one had yet shot over this reef. Clouds of blue-headed wrasse were feeding in my shadow: I paused for a long inspection, hoping to catch sight of one of the juvenile females, who mate in schools, in

the process of growing into a much larger, red-and-yellow, monogamous male. Until recently these two forms had been considered separate species, and I never see them without wondering what our own social system would be like had humans evolved with this trait.

Imagine our world, if all the senior males, the O. J. Simpsons, the Walter Cronkites and Leonid Brezhnevs, had started out as little girls and young mothers? Just in time, I remembered not to chuckle and choke myself.

Never had the underwater world been more ravishing; I flippered lazily through turquoise and liquid air, noting that the light was now tinged with faint gold. Even the evil head of a moray eel protruding from its hole in the reef was a green-gold heraldic emblem of villainy, and the enormous grouper stupidly eyeing me from a half–spear shot away was crusted with jewels.

The sea was so calm that I decided to cross the inner reef and have a look at the coral heads where the so-called sleeping sharks occasionally hide. I had acquired companions; three young barracudas were circling me, disappearing for moments only to rejoin me from a new angle, their mouths as usual open in toothy gapes. I had taken the normal precaution of removing all shiny gear, even to my medical-plaque chain, but one larger fellow was showing so much interest in my diving watch that I debated hiding it in my suit. The local barracudas are said to be harmless; I had been instructed, when meeting one nose-to-nose under water, to shout "Boo!" But I had found this difficult, especially in a snorkel mask. My sound came out as a pallid "Urk!"

I found a pass in the inner reef and flippered through, momentarily losing my carnivorous friends. The in-shore bay was an uninteresting grass-plain relieved here and there by a giant

orange starfish, a flotilla of yellowtails, or a huge live conch. It was the isolated brain-coral heads which interested me. I cruised along up-current; the old learn quickly to start their journeys upwind or uphill, so that nature will help them home. What I was looking for was a large pile with a cave at its base in which a sleeper shark might lie.

Most were too small, so I swam out farther, toward the second reef. From here I could just glimpse the shining white dot above the hazy southern coastline which was the white tower of Tuluum, high on its cliff. Tuluum is our chief local *ruina*, a mediocre remnant of greatness whose claims to fame are its glorious site and one strange carving, unique in all Yucatán, which may – or may not – concern this tale.

By the centre of the second reef I spotted exactly what I was looking for: it was perfect – great rounded boulders, with a big dim cave or tunnel at the base like those where I had encountered the sleepers in younger days, before my trick ear took the deeper dives away. This one was only about five metres down. Peering, I was almost sure that the sun was lighting something rounded and amber-tan floating in the cave. Moreover, my attendant barracudas seemed to have found business elsewhere. Could I dive down and look?

Debating, I took off my mask to clean it and noticed that the sun was now definitely slanting down. There was not much time for the long return. Dilemma: I longed mightily to look at that shark, and I longed mightily not to. It was not merely the pain I would suffer in my ear – to tell the truth, it was a lonesome place and time, if this happened to be shark wake-up hour. But – that gnawing question of my life – was I needlessly afraid? Was I, er, chicken?

As I dithered, two things occurred almost at once. The first

was auditory—I heard the beat of a boat's motor around the point. This drove the shark from my mind—there is no shame in taking refuge from the occasional maniac who tears full speed along the inner reef to make time, trusting to the god of machismo that he won't hit a coral head. Many of them also enjoy making swimmers dive for their lives. I paddled as fast as I could go for the white water of the middle reef, feeling like a wheelchair driver caught on the Indianapolis raceway.

Here I met with the second, larger event: at the base of the big reef was something long and thin and moving. The water was roiled, and at first I thought I was seeing some unearthly endless centipede, walking south. Then a clear interval showed me what it was—*langostas*, the tropic lobsters—an enormous unending file of them, all sizes and ages, following each other along the base of the reef. I was looking upon a recently discovered mystery—the Migration of the Lobsters, coming from god knew where, en route to an equally unknown destination, upon which few people have ever set eyes.

I stared, counting to the hundreds, before I came out of my trance to realise that no rooster-tailed sportscraft had appeared. In fact, now I could hear clearer, it was not a speedboat at all, but the throbbing of a much larger craft moving along the outermost reef. Correct: around the point was coming the ramshackle box-form of a *langostera*—a lobster boat—her white paint looking deceptively smart in the afternoon sun, and her old motor setting up an out-of-synch cacophony. She was towing a pair of dinghies.

The uproar ceased as she came opposite me by the far reef; there was a rattle of anchor-chain, and the dinghies were double-manned and cutting alongside the reef with unusual speed. As the nearest anchored, a figure in bright red shorts stood up and tossed his long hair before masking up. Unmistakable.

"Lorenzo! Lorenzo Canséco! ¿Qué tal?"

Typically, he gave me an offhand wave; he had long since spotted and identified me. Lorenzo was one of our local diving superstars, which meant that the *langostera* was the *Angélique*. I knew her captain well.

But there was less than the usual gaiety to Lorenzo's wave, and he was in the water fast and businesslike. The other diver, whom I hadn't seen clearly, was already in and working. The far boat was empty too. All four divers were searching the outer reef and the space between, normally a source.

I looked down at my procession of strange little beings. So long as no one crossed the middle reef in the right spot they were safe.

I swam over to Lorenzo's dinghy, a plan forming in my mind. The other diver was just coming up to boat two undersized *langostas* and a respectable grouper. To my surprise, it was my friend the owner-captain himself, an emaciated gold-tanned figure with white hair and a remarkably distinguished white hairline mustache.

"Don Manuel! *Se recuerda de su viejo amigo?*"

My Spanish has been called *únicamente desastroso*; it was possibly that, rather than my appearance, which enabled him to greet me with warmth. Then he rested his elbows on the gunwales, and I saw that he was quite tired. This probably meant that he had engaged in exertions that would have hospitalised most *gringos*.

"How goes it?"

Captain Manuel shook his white head, baring his teeth in a combined grimace of despair, fatalism, and hate. He seemed content to chat a moment while he rested. So I asked him more.

He had, it seemed, been all the way to Punta Rosa, starting before light.

"Good catch, I hope?" (But I had already noticed that the *Angélique* was riding much too high in the water.)

Manuel made an untranslatable remark, the essence of which was that one Carlos Negrón *and* his new boat could have sexual congress with the devil. It seemed that Carlos had outrun him down the entire route, preempting all the choicest spots, and at one point even side-swiping Manuel's dinghy.

"The irony of it is, Carlos doesn't even know where to fish. He is new. But he hired that *loco* Arturo whom I fired for drunkenness, may the devil screw them both. After all I put up with from Arturo, teaching him. . . ."

"A bad trip. I am grieved."

He stared sombrely at the *Angélique*, his thin face a stoic mask.

"Worse than that. I have not made even the diesel bill. And I had to place so much hope on this trip."

"There is need?"

He tossed his white hair back proudly; I could see him considering scornfully what a *gringo* could know of need. But our long friendship prevailed.

"There is need," he said simply. Nodding his head. *"Muchas dificultades en la casa. Mi niña*—my little girl, and my wife, both they are sick. They require *especialistas*, you understand. *Muy pronto.* With the government nothing can be done."

During this interchange the vision of my helpless lobsters, streaming by two hundred metres inshore, had been rising unwelcomely behind my eyes. Marching in their thousands, on the mysterious journey that had gone on since long before the

trivial race of man. A journey that was, perhaps, essential to their survival. Elsewhere they were already heavily overfished; perhaps even now they too faced their end.

But the trivial race of man was my race, and Manuel was my friend. The threat to him and his was real too. Still—had I not been there by chance, would not Manuel's own expertise have had to suffice? Nor would I have known of Carlos Negrón, nor the illness of Manuel's family.

While I floated there in the beauty, miserable, the other dinghy came up. A boy named Ruffino captained it. "*Nada*," he said, gesturing expressively. "And the petrol begins to lack. We go?"

Captain Manuel let his eyes droop closed for a moment, an expression of despair I had not before seen on his strong face. And at that moment a thought occurred to me:

"My" lobsters were not safe—not safe at all. They were headed straight toward the nets and spears of the predatory Carlos when they rounded Punta Rosa—not to mention the depredations that would be made by casual pot-hunters for a hundred miles.

"Wait, Manuel," I said. "Tell them to wait. I want you to follow me over there." I pointed to the inner reef, thinking there was just enough time to take at least a few to do him some good. The feeling of Judas choked my throat; I had to clear my snorkel twice before we were looking down at the great horde of marchers, lit by the inshore sun.

Time . . . but I had not counted on Maya speed and endurance, nor the sharp Maya eyesight—nor the underwater *focos* Manuel and Ruffino carried to light the scene.

The *Angélique* was moved twice before it was over, deep in the water and groaning in every ancient timber when Manuel called it a day.

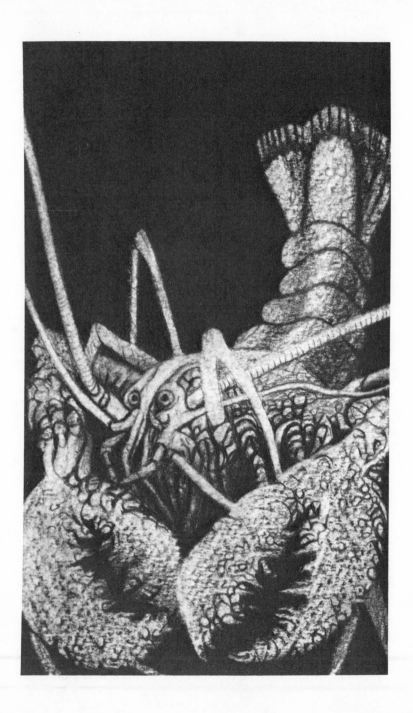

"How can I ever thank you, my friend?" Manuel inquired as the dinghies were hoisted and the *Angélique* prepared to depart. "You will wish Lorenzo to carry you back to the *rancho* in the skiff?"

"No. Many thanks, but I would prefer to go with you to Cozumel tonight. I have a small *negocio* to do in the morning. If you could perhaps lend me a shirt and help me get to the Maya Cozumel? I keep an old *maleta* of clothes with Señora Blaustein."

Manuel nodded approvingly. The Maya Cozumel is not one of your tourist palaces, but a sober and inexpensive Mexican commercial travellers' inn, run by one of the formidable Hispanic-Teutons who conduct much of Mexico's invisible commercial life.

"It would be my pleasure," said Manuel. "But the *rancho* will be searching for you, no?"

"Ah, but Don Pa'o has now a short-wave radio, on which they must listen for the Guardia Aéreo for an hour at nine every night. If you could change crystals and tell him to pick me up at the Playa del Carmen ferry tomorrow morning? You could say you fished me from the sea, to avoid trouble with the Guardia."

"Oh, no problem. Everybody uses that band to sell a motor and buy two ducks. This is an excellent idea, my friend. But you will not stay at the Maya. You will come home with me to celebrate."

"We will plan that later, Don Manuel old friend; you know I have not your strength for celebration and you will need to see to your wife."

And so it came about that Don Manuel and I reclined upon the bridge on the *Angélique*, while she creaked and grumbled her way across the moonlit straits toward Cozumel. The other divers, after a cold meal of snapper seasoned with what tasted like live coals, had promptly made for their hammocks. Don Manuel was doubtless twice as tired, but pride compelled him to take the captain's watch. The sea was quiet now, but nothing in the Quintana Roo is to be granted perfect trust.

To help him stay awake, we chatted idly in our usual mixture of tongues: of doings of mutual friends, of the iniquity of government, of all that had changed since the days when he was a young sports-boat captain and I an eager lover of the sea. His English was only somewhat better than my Spanish, but we had always understood one another well, and the tale that follows reflects that understanding as much as the literal words.

We were commenting on the skills of the various divers, notably that of Lorenzo, his head boy.

"Ah, yes. Lorenzo Canséco. He is good, very good. But the boy you should have seen was K'o." Manuel nodded, and repeated with special relish and the full Maya click:

"Aúdomaro K'o. *Mayo puro*, you understand; he was proud of it even then. K'o, K'ou—it means something like Lord, or young god, maybe. We were boys together, you see, in those days when the scuba was just getting started here." Manuel chuckled, shaking his head. "No one had ever heard of safety; we tied our gear on with sisal ropes. But K'o—he was the first to buy a proper watch. There will never be his like again."

"He is . . . gone?"

Captain Manuel hesitated and let himself make one of his few Maya mannerisms, a high-pitched sound deep in his throat. He belonged to the old school, before it became fashionable to be more Maya than Spanish. "Yes, he is gone," he said finally. "I saw him go. But . . ."

"A diving accident?"

"Oh, no. You must understand that K'o never had accidents. He was strong, he was handsome, he could do anything—but he had also the *cabeza*." Manuel tapped his forehead. "Others did foolish things—not he. I tell you: incredible— Once, below a hundred metres, his companion's airhose broke, and K'o brought him up safely, holding his own mask on the boy, back on himself, then back on the boy—all the time using his watch, so that they would not get the bends. It took nearly an hour like that to bring them both safely up. And the sea bad and night falling. I ask you—who could do that? And then the next week, Marco, the damn fool he saved, went down to two hundred and caught the rapture of the deeps. He untied himself before we knew. The last we saw of Marco, he was diving down, down into the Cuba current that runs off the north reef. We could see his light for a short time, going ever deeper and faster. Then it vanished. Even his body was never found."

"God."

"Yes. Oh, there are endless stories about K'o. He was *good*. When the *Capitan* Cousteau came through here, he chose K'o to dive with him. *De veras*. But the most funny story was about the cinema people, when K'o played the shark with the girl."

"What?"

"Yes. Everyone was crazy then, you understand, and the cinema people were *loco loquísimo*. In this story a beautiful young actress is pursued by a shark who catches her and—" Captain Manuel glanced at me expressively "—the shark, ah, makes love to her. Can you imagine? Well, they fixed K'o up in this shark body and he pursued the girl—she was a *puta*, but a beauty, the director's girl. K'o caught her all right—and then, by god, he actually did the business. Right there in the

water. In that crazy shark outfit. He just barely kept the girl from drowning, too, she was screeching like a *perico*. And the director jumping up and down in the boat — nothing he could do except howl and scream and fire K'o, who did not give a damn. I always wanted to see that film. But I think something went wrong with the camera, everyone was laughing like lunatics."

We were both chuckling too, while the old boat thudded on, following the rising moon. A school of porpoises was playing in the bow wave, their phosphorescent trails vying with the moonlight. Behind us the moonlit spark that was Tuluum was sinking out of sight. It was the last hour of true night, before the sky beyond Cozumel, island of sunrise, would fade to grey.

On the strength of the movie starlet's fate I decided to try a highly diluted sample of the good captain's fiery tequila, while he had his normal libation.

"Ah, yes, stories of youth," the old man said when we were settled again. "We were young, life was to spend. So many gone. I remember one that scared us all, though. We were exploring the great reef that slants down to the north — the one Marco jumped off into the deep — and something went wrong with this other boy's tank. His companion — not K'o — panicked and cut him loose, and poor Pedro shot to the surface like a bullet. K'o was in the boat. We pulled him in; he seemed all right but he was dead, you understand. He knew he only had a few minutes. He sent messages to his mother and sister, and then, just as the nitrogen was starting to work on him, he gave K'o his watch. It was a cheap little thing, I remember it well, because K'o always wore it, on his left wrist. Then of course the sickness took him, every cell in Pedro's body began to rupture and collapse, and the boy screaming, screaming; like a screaming bag of jelly toward the end. . . . I tell you, we were all a bit

more sober after that."

"Dreadful indeed . . . but K'o, what of him?"

"Ah . . ." The old man took a long pull at his tequila. "Well, by this time there were coming the tourists, you know, and all sorts of new equipment, and good boats. And the aqua skis. Well! If only you could have seen K'o perform on waterskis— dance, jump, stand on his head, ride one like a surfboard, carry girls—anything. And I remember he had the first of those *brillante* striped shorts, what they call Madras. The *turistas*— all the women—were falling over him. But it was no use. K'o was for the sea. Only the sea. Anything to do with the sea, he was interested—but beyond that," Manuel made the Maya

sound again— "there were many unhappy girls, I tell you. What K'o wanted he took, and then he was off again like a god.

"It was the time when the waterskiing was the great thing. *Estiloso*. K'o liked me because I always had a boat. Sometimes I could beg or borrow even a really big one. Also, I would spend the hours he wanted to perfect each thing. And then he told me what he really planned.

"He wanted to be the first man to waterski from Cozumel to the mainland. These days, perhaps, it may not sound like much, but even now it would take great strength. And with the equipment we had then—!"

"There's always a hell of a chop—very rough water in that strait."

"Yes . . . but we were young and crazy. And, moreover, he didn't plan to go straight across the shortest way. He wanted to go slightly south, up-current, to land at Tuluum. It was not stupid; the angle of the big swells would be better so.

"Of course there were no people at Tuluum then. That was before the Mexican *arqueólogos* and the *turistas*. Even the vandals, the *ladrónes*, could find nothing more to take. Soon it would have been all gone. And yet, when Chichén and Uxmal were already long dead, Tuluum was still a major place, with sea commerce and many towers and people. But not religious, I think . . . Something always a little *misterioso* about Tuluum. Barren women still sometimes make pilgrimages there to watch the sunrise. They use the old name, Zama, the Dawn."

"Poor old Tuluum," I sighed. "Have you read what the *conquistador* Grijalva said of it, when he sailed by in 1518? He did not land, you know, they found the great bay of Ascensión instead."

"No. What of Tuluum?"

" 'We saw there a shining bourg, so large that Seville itself could not have appeared larger or finer.' And he speaks of a 'very high tower, and crowds of Indians bearing standards.'"

"That . . . I had not heard." Captain Manuel's gaze was on me, yet not quite focused. "White . . . finer than Seville." He repeated so softly that I thought he might be yielding to sleep.

"So you tried this trip, this crossing?"

He blinked, nodded. "Ah, *sí!*

"It was still dark when we started, just such a morning as this is going to be, with a small moon in the sunrise. I had got hold of the best boat I knew—about seven metres with two hundred-horsepower outboards—very modern for her day. And how we worked on the ropes and harnesses—I tell you, we could have dragged wild horses. Spare skis, of course, in case one cracked or he hit flotsam. Even some candy bars and water we tied around his waist. So we crept out of the marina, in the moonlight, and he waved me on impatiently and got up on the skis, and I opened the throttle and the boat began to plane. Oh god, we were young. And the strange thing is, although K'o was so determined to be the first, he told no one but me his plans. It was all between him and the sea, I think.

"Well, for a long time it was just work, with the world turning pale around us, and me trying to pick the best path for him. He was all business, after one flourish when we took off. He just settled down determined to do it. The porpoises found us in the first light. I could see them playing around him. But that was all right; they seemed to understand the business, they never got in the way. The light was quite deceptive when we crossed the first big rough current, and I was worried that he was having a bad trip, but every time I looked back he waved me on.

"And then of course the colour began to come—a beautiful dawn—look, there's a little *róseo* ahead of us now—and our spirits rose. Of course we were headed away from the sun. But you know the west is beautiful in the sunrise too."

My Spanish was not up to attempting "Not by eastern windows only, when daylight comes, comes in the light," so I merely agreed.

"We crossed the second bad current then in good style and came to quite a stretch of smooth water. I decided it was time for him to eat and drink. So I steadied down the pace, gesturing to him. He didn't want to—he got mad and made a fist, waving me on—but I was stubborn too, and he saw I wouldn't pick up until he'd taken something. So he did, while I took the steadiest course I could. I was watching him too, to make sure he ate—I can still recall seeing the light flash off both those watches, his own good one and the poor thing the dead boy gave him on his other wrist.

"Then he threw the empty canteen away and waved me on, and I stood the boat up and we made wonderful time across that smooth sea. The sky was fantastic above us—like cities of all colours, how do you say, castles—*ciudades del cielo*, cities of the sky; and all coloured flowers with the great *rayos* of light streaming onto them from behind us, out of the east. And then just as we came through the last rough current, I saw that the lowest line of colour was the cocos of the mainland shore! And there above on the cliff was the shining tower of Tuluum, and I knew if I was careful we were really going to make it.

"But we were not there yet, not by much. Many bones of ships and men lie between where we were and the Castle of Tuluum.

"That rough water goes all the way to the main reef in front

of Tuluum, you see, sweeping along by the harbour passes; it can be malicious. And the passes are not simple; there appear to be several, although only two are truly good. But the light was brighter every moment, and the seeing was clear—I tell you, I ran those last kilometres with so great care, trying to put K'o just right of every wave—I was like a *borracho*, a drunkard, who is carrying the last bottle of tequila on earth. Whenever I looked back, he was waving to go faster. And in fact he was right, some speed is necessary for such water. But always I was worried because we would have to slow down for the pass, and the danger of the following waves broaching me—I was in such a state I was not even sure I could find the right pass, though I knew it like my wife's ear. And, oh!—the beautiful colours of the dawn, and the dolphins playing—never shall I feel such an hour again. But we were going fast, so fast.

"I had to lose speed without letting any slack come in K'o's lines, you see. But of course he understood that as well as I did. I could see him commencing to cross the wake, back and forth, always with the lines so beautifully tight, but gentle. But always waving to me to go faster, waving like mad. I thought he was for the first time a little *loco*. And then, my god—just as I found the start of the main pass, I saw him cut far to one side and I understood what he was planning.

"He was not going to follow me through, see? He was going to shoot along beside me through the *other* pass. That was why he wanted the speed. So I opened the throttle, not caring if I smashed the whole boat, and the lines went tight, tight, with the speed he needed. And yet, my god, how tired his arms must have been.

"So he turned and came snapping back past me in a great curve, like the end of a whip—standing up like a prince—I tell

you. He even waved as he shot by into his pass, on the crest of a wave, just right—did I tell you he had learned to use the skis like a surfboard, long before the surfers ever came? I could see him as clearly as I can see you, and his lines were still tight, just right—and his dolphins tearing along with him too.

"It was that strange moment of sunrise, the instant when the sun rises falsely— Oh, yes, I know how we see it by refraction before it is truly there, while it is still really under the curve of the sea. And sometimes it is the wrong shape, misshapen— although it is the true sun, still it is for a few seconds *siniestro*. A *momento espectral*—which I do not quite like. This was the sun that burst upon him just as he passed in. I remember there was a small cloud cutting it in three fat chunks, like a papaya, cold but beautiful. And at that moment K'o's harness went weird—it was still tight, you understand, and I could see him holding it—but the part near me faded in an abnormal fashion, it became hazy like a *vapor*.

"And then so many things happened to me at once, although I never took my eyes off K'o. He was planing, or riding at tremendous speed through the pass into Tuluum harbour. He had to be heading for a terrible spill in the coral. For a time he seemed still to hold the rope; for all I know the dolphins were pulling him. The wave cresting all around him—but he was still upright, tearing along in a great blaze of sun despite the crash that had to be coming. And then I noticed there was no more rope. He was holding his body like a surfer, but somehow different. Superb till the end."

Don Manuel's tone grew low and quieter, with a great seriousness. "My friend, I could not swear to you that he was not standing or riding on the dolphins, driving straight for shore. But the shore had become strange too. There was not only one *Castillo* above us, there were more. And I think in one glimpse I saw work going on—not the miserable scaffolds of the *arqueólogos*, but like building, fresh and new. And voices, people shouting, Mayas rushing down the cliff path now, rushing into the sea toward K'o. And all strangely dressed, or rather, ornamented—everything shining, colourful. But then I had no more time to look. Because you see both my motors had died.

"Oh, yes. Just as I saw him pass into the harbour, first one engine quit and then the other, dead as dogs, and I was being whirled round and carried across the pass entrance. Luckily— maybe unluckily—the tide was running out and took me with it. I was so crazy with confusion and *contra-natura*, things turned against nature—I did not even comprehend my own danger. Only I had the sense to seize the *palo* and push away from the most dangerous rocks—all the time the current and the tide were carrying me away—away—

"I had one last look at the glory—how did the man of old say it? Towers shining, noble as Seville? As it must have appeared so many hundreds of years ago, perhaps before it was ever seen by accursed eyes." For an instant the old Maya-mestizo, who normally called himself a Spaniard, allowed a hate I had never heard before to show. "Yes, and then when I could look again, there was nothing but our poor old Tuluum.

"Zama, the city of the dawn, was gone forever. And K'o with it."

Here Don Manuel got up, poured himself another tequila, and I joined him in a weaker potion. The divers were still sleeping soundly in their *amacas*, one in every corner; from two of them came gentle snores. The sky was brightening, blooming into beauty, with a great salmon explosion ahead of us, in which lay Cozumel. I glanced back at the west; again there were the glowing cities of the sky, lavender and saffron and rose, with the faint chip of setting moon still sharply visible, and somehow alien among the softness.

"No," said Don Manuel, though I had not spoken. "Nothing of him was ever found. No body, no skis, not a scrap, nothing. Although everyone looked for weeks, even from the air. And—another strange thing—even the coil of rope-end in my *lancha* was gone too. I remember in the excitement I had glimpsed it seeming faint, like a mist, but I was too busy trying to save myself from wrecking to attend to that."

"How did you come ashore?"

"Well, I tell you, I thought I was going to Cuba. I was sure there was water or dirt in the petrol, you see, although we had strained it three times through a good *lana* hat. Oh, he overlooked nothing, that K'o! So I was sucking and blowing away, drinking petrol so I was sick, when suddenly the motor started

quite normally, and then the other, which I had not even touched. So I tore right back, looking for K'o—I went into the harbour, everywhere—but there was nothing but our dead ruined old Tuluum. And one *viejo*, a sort of caretaker, who had been shooting doves. He said he had heard a motor, but he was in the *mangles* after *palomas*, he had seen nothing. ¡*Nada!* And he crossed himself—" here Don Manuel made a comic gesture— "about twenty times.

"I went back to Cozumel—the motors ran perfectly. And of course I alerted the Guardia, and all K'o's friends. But there was nothing, nothing, nothing, nothing. Nothing except one thing only, which I know. Shall I tell you a strangeness, my friend?"

"You ask me? May you never find another *langosta* if you keep silent now."

"Very well." He took a deep, deep draught. "This I never told. You know our poor Tuluum, how it is famous for two things. One is of course the magnificent site, the wall and the view from the *Castillo*, correct? And do you know the other, which is in every stupid guidebook?"

"What? Not the frescoes, they are gone. A few *Chacs*, rain gods— Oh! Of course. The figure over the top door, the Descending God, or whatever you will."

"Do you know it is the only such a one in all Yucatán? In no other Maya *ruina*, even Tikal. Some fools call it the Descending God, or a setting sun, such as a few Aztec temples have up in Mexico. But this one is quite, quite different. I have made it my business to compare, you see. Even from the oldest drawings before the vandals came. You can believe me. The posture is not elegant, indeed, it is somewhat like a frog. Nevertheless,

everyone except some of the *arqueólogos* call it not descending, but the *diving* god. The vandals have been at it, and the weather, of course. But I have consulted the old drawings, like your Catherwoods from Stephens's books. Have you never examined these?"

"No, not really."

"Well. Some are very detailed. The hands are held so—" Don Manuel put his fingers together like a diving child. "And on the wrists he drew stiff cuffs with ruffles. But these are only drawn to fill the space, I think, it was already damaged, you see. Such cuffs are never seen elsewhere. Like Spanish court cuffs, or the cuffs the little *typistas* wear to keep their sleeves clean. The real statue that you can see today has no trace of such things. But if you look carefully you can see there was indeed something there, upon the wrists. Very *ornamentales*. But not big cuffs. One perhaps a little smaller than the other, on the left wrist. And by the wrists—you know the Maya symbols for numbers, the bars and dots, not so?"

"Yes."

"Well, a few small ones can still be made out, in the space by the diving hands. Strange wrist ornaments—figures of time? . . . How would the ancients show a diver's watch, I ask you?"

"Oh, my god, Manuel."

"Exactly, my friend. His name too, did you forget? K'o, K'ou, a god!"

There fell then a long silence, in which I became slowly conscious of the uproar of the old engines, the groans, the creaks, the double snore . . . the dawn wind, broken by an osprey's scream . . . the glorious sunrise over the marina pier, now visible ahead, from which came the almost imperceptible tinkle of a mariachi from some early riser's radio.

Presently I sighed. "So you really think he made it, Don Manuel?"

"I know what I have seen, my friend," Manuel said quietly. "And every word I have told you is the truth. I believe he was indeed the first man to waterski from Cozumel to the mainland. By several hundreds—perhaps, who knows?—even a thousand years. *Mil años, más o menos. ¿Quién sabe?*"

A lust death-born, unsated,
Calls from a poisoned bed;
Where monsters half-created
Writhe, unliving and undead.
None know for what they're fated,
None know on what they've fed.

Beyond the Dead Reef

My informant was, of course, spectacularly unreliable.

The only character reference I have for him comes from the intangible nuances of a small restaurant-owner's remarks, and the only confirmation of his tale lies in the fact that an illiterate fishing-guide appears to believe it. If I were to recount all the reasons why no sane mind should take it seriously, we could never begin. So I will only report the fact that today I found myself shuddering with terror when a perfectly innocent sheet of seaworn plastic came slithering over my snorkelling-reef, as dozens have done for years—and get on with the story.

I met him one evening this December at the Cozumel *Buzo*, on my first annual supply trip. As usual, the *Buzo*'s outer rooms were jammed with tourist divers and their retinues and gear. That's standard. *El Buzo* means, roughly, The Diving, and the *Buzo* is their place. Marcial's big sign in the window reads "DIVVERS UELCOME! BRING YR FISH WE COK WITH CAR. FIRST DRINK FREE!"

Until he went in for the "Divvers," Marcial's had been a small quiet place where certain delicacies like stone-crab could be at least semi-legally obtained. Now he did a roaring trade in snappers and groupers cooked to order at outrageous fees, with a flourishing sideline in fresh fish sales to the neighbourhood each morning.

The "roaring" was quite literal. I threaded my way through a crush of burly giants and giantesses of all degrees of naked-ness, hairiness, age, proficiency, and inebriation—all eager to

share their experiences and plans in voices powered by scuba-deafened ears and Marcial's free drink, beneath which the sound-system could scarcely be heard at full blast. (Marcial's only real expense lay in first-drink liquor so strong that few could recall whether what they ultimately ate bore any resemblance to what they had given him to cook.) Only a handful were sitting down yet, and the amount of gear underfoot and on the walls would have stocked three sports shops. This was not mere exhibitionism; on an island chronically short of washers, valves, and other spare parts the diver who lets his gear out of his sight is apt to find it missing in some vital.

I paused to allow a young lady to complete her massage of the neck of a youth across the aisle who was deep in talk with three others, and had time to notice the extraordinary number of heavy spear-guns racked about. Oklahomans, I judged, or perhaps South Florida. But then I caught clipped New England from the centre group. Too bad; the killing mania seems to be spreading yearly, and the armament growing ever more menacing and efficient. When I inspected their platters, however, I saw the usual array of lavishly garnished lobsters and common fish. At least they had not yet discovered what to eat.

The mermaiden blocking me completed her task—unthanked—and I continued on my way in the little inner sanctum Marcial keeps for his old clientele. As the heavy doors cut off the uproar, I saw that this room was full too—three tables of dark-suited Mexican businessmen and a decorous family of eight, all quietly intent on their plates. A lone customer sat at the small table by the kitchen door, leaving an empty seat and a child's chair. He was a tall, slightly balding Anglo some years younger than I, in a very decent sports jacket. I recalled having seen him about now and then on my banking and shopping trips to

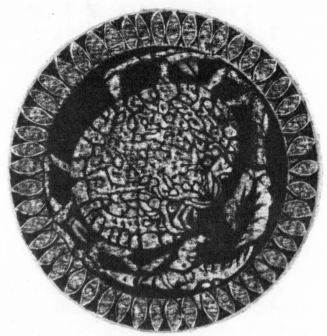

the island.

Marcial telegraphed me a go-ahead nod as he passed through laden with more drinks, so I approached.

"Mind if I join you?"

He looked up from his stone-crab and gave me a slow, owlish smile.

"Welcome. A *diverse* welcome," he enunciated carefully. The accent was vaguely British, yet agreeable. I also perceived that he was extremely drunk, but in no common way.

"Thanks."

As I sat down I saw that he was a diver too, but his gear was stowed so unobtrusively I hadn't noticed it. I tried to stack my own modest snorkel outfit neatly, pleased to note that, like me, he seemed to carry no spear-gun. He watched me attentively, blinking once or twice, and then returned to an exquisitely exact dissection of his stone-crab.

When Marcial brought my own platter of crab—unasked—
we engaged in our ritual converse. Marcial's English is several
orders of magnitude better than my Spanish, but he always
does me the delicate courtesy of allowing me to use his tongue.
How did I find my rented *casita* on the coco ranch this year?
Fine. How goes the tourist business this year? Fine. I learn from
Marcial: the slight pause before his answer in a certain tone,
meant that in fact the tourist business was lousy so far, but
would hopefully pick up; I used the same to convey that in
fact my *casa* was in horrible shape but reparable. I tried to cheer
him by saying that I thought the *Buzo* would do better than
the general *turismo*, because the diving enthusiasm was spreading in the States. "True," he conceded. "So long as they don't
discover the other places—like Bélizé." Here he flicked a glance
at my companion, who gave his solemn blink. I remarked that
my country's politics were in disastrous disarray, and he conceded the same for his; the *Presidente* and his pals had just
made off with much of the nation's treasury. And I expressed
the hope that Mexico's new oil would soon prove a great boon.
"Ah, but it will be a long time before it gets to the little people
like us," said Marcial, with so much more than his normal
acerbity that I refrained from my usual joke about his having
a Swiss bank account. The uproar from the outer rooms had
risen several decibels, but just before Marcial had to leave he
paused and said in a totally different voice, "My grandson
Antonito Vincente has four teeth!"

His emotion was so profound that I seized his free hand and
shook it lightly, congratulating him in English. And then he was
gone, taking on his "Mexican waiter" persona quite visibly as
he passed the inner doors.

As we resumed our attention to the succulence before us,

my companion said in his low, careful voice, "Nice chap, Marcial. He likes you."

"It's mutual," I told him between delicate mouthfuls. Stone-crab is not to be gulped. "Perhaps because I'm old enough to respect the limits where friendship ends and the necessities of life take over."

"I say, that's rather good," my companion chuckled. "Respect for the limits where friendship ends and the necessities of life take over, eh? Very few Yanks do, you know. At least the ones we see down here."

His speech was almost unslurred, and there were no drinks before him on the table. We chatted idly a bit more. It was becoming apparent that we would finish simultaneously and be faced with the prospect of leaving together, which could be awkward, if he, like me, had no definite plans for the evening.

The dilemma was solved when my companion excused himself momentarily just as Marcial happened by.

I nodded to his empty chair. "Is he one of your old customers, Señor Marcial?"

As always Marcial understood the situation at once. "One of the oldest," he told me, and added low-voiced, "*muy buenes gentes* — a really good guy. *Un poco de dificultades* —" he made an almost imperceptible gesture of drinking — "but *controlado*. And he has also *negocios* — I do not know all, but some are important for his country. — So you really like the crab?" he concluded in his normal voice. "We are honoured."

My companion was emerging from the rather dubious regions that held the *excusado*.

Marcial's recommendation was good enough for me. Only one puzzle remained: what was his country? As we both refused *dulce* and coffee, I suggested that he might care to stroll down

to the marina with me and watch the sunset.

"Good thought."

We paid up Marcial's outrageous bills and made our way through the exterior Bedlam, carrying our gear. One of the customers was brandishing his spear-gun as he protested his bill. Marcial seemed to have lost all his English except the words

"Police," and cooler heads were attempting to calm the irate one. "All in a night's work," my companion commented as we emerged into a blaze of golden light.

The marina to our left was a simple L-shaped *muelle*, or pier, still used by everything from dinghies to commercial fishermen and baby yachts. It will be a pity when and if the town decides to separate the sports tourist-trade from the more interesting working craft. As we walked out toward the pier in the last spectacular colour of the tropic sunset over the mainland, the rigging lights of a cruise ship standing out in the channel came on, a fairyland illusion over the all-too-dreary reality.

"They'll be dumping and cleaning out their used bunkers tonight," my companion said, slurring a trifle now. He had a congenial walking gait, long-strided but leisurely. I had the impression that his drunkenness had returned slightly; perhaps the fresh air. "Damn crime."

"I couldn't agree more," I told him. "I remember when we used to start snorkelling and scuba-diving right off the shore here—you could almost wade out to untouched reefs. And now—"

There was no need to look; one could smell it. The effluvia of half a dozen hotels and the town behind ran out of pipes that were barely covered at low tide; only a few parrot-fish, who can stand anything, remained by the hotel-side restaurants to feed on the crusts the tourists threw them from their tables. And only the very ignorant would try out—once—the dilapidated Sunfish and water-ski renters who plied the small stretches of beach between hotels.

We sat down on one of the near benches to watch a commercial trawler haul net. I had been for some time aware that my companion, while of largely British culture, was not completely Caucasian. There was a minute softness to the voice, a something not quite dusky about hair and fingernails—not so much as to be what in my youth was called "A touch of the tarbrush," but nothing that originated in Yorkshire, either. Nor was it the obvious Hispano-Indian. I recollected Marcial's earlier speech and enlightenment came.

"Would I be correct in taking Marcial's allusions to mean that you are a British Honduran—forgive me, I mean a Bélizéian, or Bélizan?"

"Nothing to forgive, old chap. We haven't existed long enough to get our adjectives straight."

"May god send you do." I was referring to the hungry maws of Guatemala and Honduras, the little country's big neighbours, who had the worst of intentions toward her. "I happen to be quite a fan of your country. I had some small dealings there after independence which involved getting all my worldly goods out of your customs on a national holiday, and people couldn't have been finer to me."

"Ah yes. Bélizé the blessed, where sixteen nationalities live in perfect racial harmony. The odd thing is, they do."

"I could see that. But I couldn't quite count all sixteen."

"My own grandmother was a Burmese—so called. I think it was the closest grandfather could come to Black. Although the mix *is* extraordinary."

"My factor there was a very dark Hindu with red hair and a Scottish accent, named Robinson. I had to hire him in seven minutes. He was a miracle of efficiency. I hope he's still going."

"Robinson . . . Used to work for customs?"

"Why, yes, now you recall it."

"He's fine. . . . Of course, we felt it when the British left. Among other things, half the WCs in the hotels broke down the first month. But there are more important things in life than plumbing."

"That I believe. . . . But you know, I've never been sure how much help the British would have been to you. Two years before your independence I called the British Embassy with a question about your immigration laws, and believe it or not I couldn't find one soul who even knew there *was* a British Honduras, let alone that they owned it. One child finally denied it flatly and hung up. And this was their main embassy in Washington, D.C. I realised then that Britain was not only sick, but crazy."

"Actually denied our existence, eh?" My companion's voice held a depth and timbre of sadness such as I have heard only from victims of better-known world wrongs. Absently his hand went under his jacket, and he pulled out something gleaming.

"Forgive me." It was a silver flask, exquisitely plain. He uncapped and drank, a mere swallow, but, I suspected, something of no ordinary power. He licked his lips as he recapped it, and sat up straighter while he put it away.

"Shall we move along out to the end?"

"With pleasure."

We strolled on, passing a few late sports-boats disgorging hungry divers.

"I'm going to do some modest exploring tomorrow," I told him. "A guide named Jorge—" in Spanish it's pronounced Hor-hay— "Jorge Chuc is taking me out to the end of the north reef. He says there's a pretty little untouched spot out there. I hope so. Today I went south, it was so badly shot over I almost wept. Cripples—and of course shark everywhere. Would you believe I found a big she-turtle, trying to live with a steel bolt through her neck? I managed to catch her, but all I could do for her was pull it out. I hope she makes it."

"Bad . . . Turtles are tough, though. If it wasn't vital you may have saved her. But did you say that Jorge Chuc is taking you to the end of the north reef?"

"Yes, why? Isn't it any good?"

"Oh, there is one pretty spot. But there's some very bad stuff there too. If you don't mind my advice, don't go far from the boat. I mean, a couple of metres. And don't follow anything. And above all be very sure it *is* Jorge's boat."

His voice had become quite different, with almost military authority.

"A couple of metres!" I expostulated. "But—"

"I know, I know. What I don't know is why Chuc is taking you there at all." He thought for a moment. "You haven't by any chance offended him, have you? In any way?"

"Why, no—we were out for a long go yesterday, and had a nice chat on the way back. Yes . . . although he is a trifle changeable, isn't he? I put it down to fatigue, and gave him some extra *dinero* for being only one party."

My companion made an untranslatable sound, compounded of dubiety, speculation, possible enlightenment, and strong suspicion.

"Did he tell you the name of that part of the reef? Or that it's out of sight of land?"

"Yes, he said it was far out. And that part of it was so poor it's called dead."

"And you chatted—forgive me, but was your talk entirely in Spanish?"

I chuckled deprecatingly. "Well, yes—I know my Spanish is pretty horrible, but he seemed to get the drift."

"Did you mention his family?"

"Oh, yes—I could draw you the whole Chuc family tree."

"Hmmm . . ." My companion's eyes had been searching the pier-side where the incoming boats were being secured for the night.

"Ah. There's Chuc now. This is none of my business, you understand—but do I have your permission for a short word with Jorge?"

"Why, yes. If you think it necessary."

"I do, my friend. I most certainly do."

"Carry on."

His long-legged stride had already carried him to Chuc's big skiff, the *Estrellita*. Chuc was covering his motors. I had raised my hand in greeting, but he was apparently too busy to respond. Now he greeted my companion briefly, but did not turn when he clambered into the boat uninvited. I could not hear the interchange. But presently the two men were standing, faces somewhat averted from each other as they conversed. My com-

panion made rather a long speech, ending with questions. There was little response from Chuc until a sudden outburst from him took me by surprise. The odd dialogue went on for some time after that; Chuc seemed to calm down. Then the tall Bélizan waved me over.

"Will you say exactly what I tell you to say?"

"Why—" But his expression stopped me. "If you say it's important."

"It is. Can you say in Spanish, 'I ask your pardon, Mr. Chuc. I mistook myself in your language. I did not say anything of what you thought I said. Please forgive my error. And please let us be friends again.'"

"I'll try."

I stumbled through the speech, which I will not try to reproduce here, as I repeated several phrases with what I thought was better accent, and I'm sure I threw several verbs into the conditional future. Before I was through, Chuc was beginning to grin. When I came to the "friends" part he had relaxed, and after a short pause, said in very tolerable English, "I see, so I accept your apology. We will indeed be friends. It was a regrettable error. . . . And I advise you, do not again speak in Spanish."

We shook on it.

"Good," said my companion. "And he'll take you out tomorrow, but not to the Dead Reef. And keep your hands off your wallet tonight, but I suggest liberality tomorrow eve."

We left Chuc to finish up, and paced down to a bench at the very end of the *muelle*. The last colours of evening, peaches and rose shot with unearthly green, were set off by a few low-lying clouds already in grey shadow, like sharks of the sky passing beneath a sentimental vision of bliss.

"Now what was all *that* about!" I demanded of my new friend. He was just tucking the flask away again, and shuddered lightly.

"I don't wish to seem overbearing, but *that* probably saved your harmless life, my friend. I repeat Jorge's advice — stay away from that Spanish of yours unless you are absolutely sure of being understood."

"I know it's ghastly."

"That's not actually the problem. The problem is that it isn't ghastly enough. Your pronunciation is quite fair, and you've mastered some good idioms, so people who don't know you think you speak more fluently than you do. In this case the trouble came from your damned rolled *rrr*s. Would you mind saying the words for 'but' and 'dog'?"

"*Pero . . . perro.* Why?"

"The difference between a rolled and a single *r*, particularly in Maya Spanish, is very slight. The upshot of it was that you not only insulted his boat in various ways, but you ended by referring to his mother as a dog. . . . He was going to take you out beyond the Dead Reef and leave you there."

"*What?*"

"Yes. And if it hadn't been I who asked—he knows I know the story—you'd never have understood a thing. Until you turned up as a statistic."

"Oh, Jesus Christ . . ."

"Yes," he said dryly.

"I guess some thanks are in order," I said finally. "But words seem a shade inadequate. Have you any suggestions?"

My companion suddenly turned and gave me a highly concentrated look.

"You were in World War Two, weren't you? And afterwards you worked around quite a bit." He wasn't asking me, so I kept quiet. "Right now, I don't see anything," he went on. "But just possibly I might be calling on you," he grinned, "with something you may not like."

"If it's anything I can do from a wheelchair, I won't forget."

"Fair enough. We'll say no more about it now."

"Oh yes, we will," I countered. "You may not know it, but you owe *me* something. I can smell a story when one smacks me in the face. What I want from you is the story behind this Dead Reef business, and how it is that Jorge knows you know something special about it. If I'm not asking too much? I'd really like to end our evening with your tale of the Dead Reef."

"Oho. My error—I'd forgotten Marcial telling me you wrote. . . . Well, I can't say I enjoy reliving it, but maybe it'll have a salutary effect on your future dealings in Spanish. The fact is, I was the one it happened to, and Jorge was driving a certain boat. You

realise, though, there's not a shred of proof except my own word? And my own word—" he tapped the pocket holding his flask "—is only as good as you happen to think it is."

"It's good enough for me."

"Very well, then. Very well," he said slowly, leaning back. "It happened about three, no, four years back—by god, you know this is hard to tell, though there's not much to it." He fished in another pocket, and took out, not a flask, but the first cigaret I'd seen him smoke, a *Petit Caporal*. "I was still up to a long day's scuba then, and, like you, I wanted to explore north. I'd run into this nice, strong, young couple who wanted the same thing. Their gear was good, they seemed experienced and sensible. So we got a third tank apiece, and hired a trustable boatman—not Jorge, Victor Camul—to take us north over the worst of the reef. It wasn't so bad then, you know.

"We would be swimming north with the current until a certain point, where if you turn east, you run into a long reverse eddy that makes it a lot easier to swim back to Cozumel. And just to be extra safe, Victor was to start out up the eddy in two hours sharp to meet us and bring us home. I hadn't one qualm about the arrangements. Even the weather cooperated—not a cloud, and the forecast perfect. Of course, if you miss up around here, the next stop is four hundred miles to Cuba, but you know that; one gets used to it. . . . By the way, have you heard they're still looking for that girl who's been gone two days on a Sunfish with no water?"

I said nothing.

"Sorry." He cleared his throat. "Well, Victor put us out well in sight of shore. We checked watches and compasses and lights. The plan was for the lad Harry to lead, Ann to follow, and me to bring up the rear. Harry had Day Glo-red shorts you could see a mile, and Ann was white-skinned with long black hair and a brilliant neon-blue-and-orange bathing suit on her little rump—you could have seen her in a mine at midnight. Even I got some yellow water safety-tape and tied it around my arse and tanks.

"The one thing we didn't have then was a radio. At the time they didn't seem worth the crazy cost, and were unreliable besides. I had no way of guessing I'd soon give my life for one— and very nearly did.

"Well, when Victor let us out and we got organised and started north single file over the dead part of the reef, we almost surfaced and yelled for him to take us back right then. It was purely awful. But we knew there was better stuff ahead, so we stuck it out and flippered doggedly along—actually doing pretty damn fair time, with the current—and trying not to look too closely at what lay below.

"Not only was the coral dead, you understand—that's where the name got started. We think now it's from oil and chemical wash, such as that pretty ship out there is about to contribute— but there was tons and tons of litter, *basura* of all description, crusted there. It's everywhere, of course—you've seen what washes onto the mainland beach—but here the current and the reef produce a particularly visible concentration. Even quite large heavy things—bedsprings, auto chassis—in addition to things you'd expect, like wrecked skiffs. Cozumel, *Basurero del Caribe!*"

He gave a short laugh, mocking the Gem-of-the-Caribbean ads, as he lit up another *Caporal*. The most polite translation of *basurero* is garbage can.

"A great deal of the older stuff was covered with that evil killer algae—you know, the big coarse red-brown hairy kind, which means that nothing else can ever grow there again. But some of the heaps were too new.

"I ended by getting fascinated and swimming lower to look, always keeping one eye on that blue-and-orange rump above

me with her white legs and black flippers. And the stuff—I don't mean just Clorox and *detergente* bottles, beer cans and netting —but weird things like about ten square metres of butchered pink plastic baby-dolls—arms and legs wiggling, and rose bud mouths—it looked like a babies' slaughter-house. Syringes, hypos galore. Fluorescent tubes on end, waving like drowned orchestra conductors. A great big red sofa with a skeletonised

banana-stem or *something* sitting in it—when I saw that, I went back up and followed right behind Ann.

"And then the sun dimmed unexpectedly, so I surfaced for a look. The shoreline was fine, we had plenty of time, and the cloud was just one of a dozen little thermals that form on a hot afternoon like this. When I went back down Ann was looking at me, so I gave her the All's Fair sign. And with that we swam over a pair of broken dories and found ourselves in a different world—the beauty patch we'd been looking for.

"The reef was live here—whatever had killed the coral hadn't reached yet, and the damned *basura* had quit or been deflected, aside from a beer bottle or two. There was life everywhere; anemones, sponges, conches, fans, stars—and fish, oh my! No one ever came here, you see. In fact, there didn't seem to have been any spearing, the fish were as tame as they used to be years back.

"Well, we began zig-zagging back and forth, just revelling in it. And every time we'd meet head-on we'd make the gesture of putting our fingers to our lips, meaning, Don't tell anyone about this, ever!

"The formation of the reef was charming, too. It broadened into a sort of big stadium, with allées and cliffs and secret pockets, and there were at least eight different kinds of coral. And most of it was shallow enough so the sunlight brought out the glorious colours—those little black-and-yellow fish—butterflies, I forget their proper name—were dazzling. I kept having to brush them off my mask, they wanted to look in.

"The two ahead seemed to be in ecstasies; I expect they hadn't seen much like this before. They swam on and on, investigating it all—and I soon realised there was real danger of losing them in some coral pass. So I stuck tight to Ann. But

time was passing. Presently I surfaced again to investigate—and, my god, the shoreline was damn near invisible and the line-up we had selected for our turn marker was all but passed! Moreover, a faint hazy overcast was rising from the west.

"So I cut down again, intending to grab Ann and start, which Harry would have to see. So I set off after the girl. I used to be a fair sprint-swimmer, but I was amazed how long it took me to catch her. I recall vaguely noticing that the reef was going a bit bad again, dead coral here and there. Finally I came right over her, signed to her to halt, and kicked up in front of her nose for another look.

"To my horror the shoreline was gone and the overcast had overtaken the sun. We would have to swim east by compass, and swim hard. I took a moment to hitch my compass around where I could see it well—it was the old-fashioned kind—and then I went back down for Ann. And the damn fool girl wasn't there. It took me a minute to locate that blue bottom and white legs; I assumed she'd gone after Harry, having clearly no idea of the urgency of our predicament.

"I confess the thought crossed my mind that I could cut out of there, and come back for them later with Victor, but this was playing a rather iffy game with someone else's lives. And if they were truly unaware, it would be fairly rotten to take off without even warning them. So I went after Ann again—my god, I can still see that blue tail and the white limbs and black feet and hair with the light getting worse every minute and the bottom now gone really rotten again. And as bad luck would have it she was going in just the worst line—north-north-west.

"Well, I swam and I swam and I *swam*. You know how a chase takes you, and somehow being unable to overtake a mere girl made it worse. But I was gaining, age and all, until just as I

got close enough to sense something was wrong, she turned sidewise above two automobile tyres—and I saw it wasn't a girl at all.

"I had been following a god-damned great fish—a fish with a bright blue-and-orange band around its belly, and a thin white body ending in a black flipperlike tail. Even its head and nape were black, like her hair and mask. It had a repulsive catfishlike mouth, with barbels.

"The thing goggled at me and then swam awkwardly away, just as the light went worse yet. But there was enough for me to see that it was no normal fish, either, but a queer archaic thing that looked more tacked together than grown. This I can't swear to, because I was looking elsewhere by then, but it was my strong impression that as it went out of my line of sight its whole tail broke off.

"But as I say, I was looking elsewhere. I had turned my light on, although I was not deep but only dim, because I had to read my watch and compass. It had just dawned on me that I was very probably a dead man. My only chance, if you can call it that, was to swim east as long as I could, hoping for that eddy and Victor. And when my light came on, the first thing I saw was the girl, stark naked and obviously stone cold dead, lying in a tangle of nets and horrid stuff on the bottom ahead.

"Of Harry or anything human there was no sign at all. But there was a kind of shining, like a pool of moonlight, around her, which was so much stronger than my lamp that I clicked it off and swam slowly toward her, through the nastiest mess of *basura* I had yet seen. The very water seemed vile. It took longer to reach her than I had expected, and soon I saw why.

"They speak of one's blood running cold with horror, y'know. Or people becoming numb with horror piled on horrors. I believe I experienced both those effects. It isn't pleasant, even now." He lit a third *Caporal*, and I could see that the smoke column trembled. Twilight had fallen while he'd been speaking. A lone mercury lamp came on at the shore end of the pier; the one near us was apparently out, but we sat in what would ordinarily have been a pleasant tropic evening, sparkling with many moving lights—whites, reds, and green, of late-moving incomers and the rainbow lighting from the jewel-lit cruise ship ahead, all cheerfully reflected in the unusually calm waters.

"Again I was mistaken, you see. It wasn't Ann at all; but the rather more distant figure of a young woman, of truly enormous size. All in this great ridge of graveyard luminosity, of garbage in phosphorescent decay. The current was carrying me slowly, inexorably, right toward her—as it had carried all that was there now. And perhaps I was also a bit hypnotised. She grew in my sight metre by metre as I neared her. I think six metres—eighteen feet—was about it, at the end. . . . I make that guess later, you understand, as an exercise in containing the unbearable—by recalling the size of known items in the junkpile she lay on. One knee, for example, lay alongside an oil drum. At the time she simply filled my world. I had no doubt she was dead, and very beautiful. One of her legs seemed to writhe gently.

"The next stage of horror came when I realised that she was not a gigantic woman at all—or rather, like the fish, she was a woman-shaped construction. The realisation came to me first, I think, when I could no longer fail to recognise that her 'breasts' were two of those great net buoys with the blue knobs for nipples.

"After that it all came with a rush—that she was a made-up body—all sorts of pieces of plastic, rope, styrofoam, netting, crates, and bolts—much of it clothed with that torn translucent white polyethylene for skin. Her hair was a dreadful tangle of something, and her crotch was explicit and unspeakable. One hand was a torn, inflated rubber glove, and her face—well, I won't go into it except that one eye was a traffic reflector and her mouth was partly a rusted can.

"Now you might think this discovery would have brought some relief, but quite the opposite. Because simultaneously I had realised the very worst thing of all—

"She was alive."

He took a long drag on his cigaret.

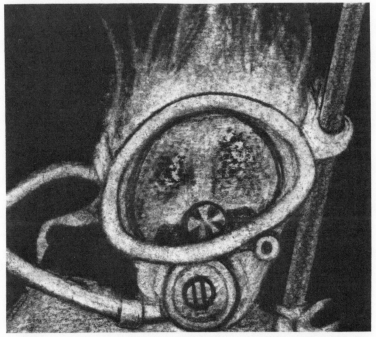

"You know how things are moved passively in water? Plants waving, a board seesawing and so on? Sometimes enough almost to give an illusion of mobile life. What I saw was nothing of this sort.

"It wasn't merely that as I floated over, her horrible eyes

'opened' and looked at me and her rusted-can mouth *smiled*.
Oh, no.

"What I mean is that as she smiled, first one whole arm,
shedding junk, stretched up and reached for me *against the
current*, and then the other did the same.

"And when I proved to be out of reach, this terrifying figure,
or creature, or unliving life, actually sat up, again *against the
current*, and reached up toward me with both arms at full
extension.

"And as she did so, one of her 'breasts' – the right one –
came loose and dangled by some tenuous thready stuff.

"All this seemed to pass in slow motion – I even had time
to see that there were other unalive yet living things moving
near her on the pile. Not fish, but more what I should have
taken, on land, for rats or vermin – and I distinctly recall the
paper-flat skeleton of something like a chicken, running and
pecking. And other moving things like nothing in this world.
I have remembered all this very carefully, y'see, from what must
have been quick glimpses, because in actual fact I was apparently
kicking like mad in a frenzied effort to get away from those
dreadful reaching arms.

"It was not till I shot to the surface with a mighty splash
that I came somewhere near my senses. Below and behind me
I could still see faint cold light. Above was twilight and the
darkness of an oncoming small storm.

"At that moment the air in my last tank gave out – or rather
that splendid Yank warning buzz, which means you have just
time to get out of your harness, sounded off.

"I had, thank god, practised the drill. Despite being a terror-
paralysed madman, habit got me out of the harness before the
tanks turned into lethal deadweight. In my panic, of course,

the headlight went down too. I was left unencumbered in the night, free to swim toward Cuba, or Cozumel, and to drown as slow or fast as fate willed.

"The little storm had left the horizon stars free. I recall that pure habit made me take a sight on what seemed to be Canopus, which should be over Cozumel. I began to swim in that direction. I was appallingly tired, and as the adrenalin of terror which had brought me this far began to fade out of my system, I realised I could soon be merely drifting, and would surely die in the next day's sun if I survived till then. Nevertheless it seemed best to swim whilst I could.

"I rather resented it when some time after a boat motor passed nearby. It forced me to attempt to yell and wave, nearly sinking myself. I was perfectly content when the boat passed on. But someone had seen—a spotlight wheeled blindingly, motors reversed, I was forcibly pulled from my grave and voices from what I take to be your Texas demanded, roaring with laughter,"—here he gave quite a creditable imitation—"'Whacha doin' out hyar, boy, this time of night? Ain't no pussy out hyar, less'n ya'all got a date with a mermaid.' They had been trolling for god knows what, mostly beer.

"The driver of that boat claimed me as a friend and later took me home for the night, where I told him—and to him alone—the whole story. He was Jorge Chuc.

"Next day I found that the young couple, Harry and Ann, had taken only a brief look at the charming unspoiled area, and then started east, exactly according to plan, with me—or something very much like me—following behind them all the way. They had been a trifle surprised at my passivity and un-communicativeness, and more so when, on meeting Victor, I was no longer to be found. But they had taken immediate

action, even set a full-scale search in progress — approximately seventy kilometres from where I then was. As soon as I came to myself I had to concoct a wild series of lies about cramps and heart trouble to get them in the clear and set their minds at ease. Needless to say, my version included no mention of diver-imitating fish-life."

He tossed the spark of his cigaret over the rail before us.

"So now, my friend, you know the whole story of all I know of what is to be found beyond the Dead Reef. It may be that others know of other happenings and developments there. Or of similar traps elsewhere. The sea is large. . . . Or it may be that the whole yarn comes from neuroses long abused by stuff like this."

I had not seen him extract his flask, but he now took two deep, shuddering swallows.

I sighed involuntarily, and then sighed again. I seemed to have been breathing rather inadequately during the end of his account.

"Ordinary thanks don't seem quite appropriate here," I finally said. "Though I do thank you. Instead I am going to make two guesses. The second is that you might prefer to sit quietly here alone, enjoying the evening, and defer the mild entertainment I was about to offer you to some other time. I'd be glad to be proved wrong . . . ?"

"No. You're very perceptive, I welcome the diverse — the deferred offer." His tongue stumbled a bit now, more from fatigue than anything he'd drunk. "But what was your first guess?"

I rose and slowly paced a few metres to and fro, remembering to pick up my absurd snorkel bag. Then I turned and gazed out to the sea.

"I can't put it into words. It has something to do with the idea that the sea is still, well, strong. Perhaps it can take revenge? No, that's too simple. I don't know. I have only a feeling that our ordinary ideas of what may be coming on us may be—oh—not deep, or broad enough. I put this poorly. But perhaps the sea, or nature, will not die passively at our hands, . . . perhaps death itself may turn or return in horrible life upon us, besides the more mechanical dooms. . . ."

"Our thoughts are not so far apart," the tall Bélizan said. "I welcome them to my night's agenda."

"To which I now leave you, unless you've changed your mind?"

He shook his head. I hoisted his bag to the seat beside him. "Don't forget this. I almost left mine."

"Thanks. And don't you forget about dogs and mothers," he grinned faintly.

"Goodnight."

My footsteps echoed on the now deserted *muelle* left him sitting there. I was quite sure he was no longer smiling.

Nor was I.

Quintana Roo, maps call it,
That blazing, blood-soaked shore;
Which brown men called *Zama*, the Dawn,
And other men called names long gone
A thousand years before.
Still songs of gold that dead men sought,
And lures of love that dieth not,
And hungry life by death begot,
Murmur from ocean's floor.